Blessings In Disguise: When Life Takes A Turn For The Worse

By Shana Johnson

Published By: TamikaINK

Library of Congress Cataloging-in-Publication Data has been applied for
ISBN: 979-8-9881046-6-7

PRINTED IN THE UNITED STATES OF AMERICA

<h1 style="text-align:center">Acknowledgments</h1>

First, I want to thank my savior Jesus Christ. I want to thank my parents for giving me the gift of Jesus because I don't know where I would be without Him, and thank you for teaching me and guiding me. I want to thank my best friend and sister for believing in me and telling me what God told her to speak to me. My children, who are my world, I love you. Thank you, babies, for helping Mommy come up with this title. I want to thank my book publishing company for taking time out of your day and working hours and hours on editing for me. Lastly, to whom this book comes across, I hope it blesses you and that you come out of whatever situation you are in because there is a Blessing in Disguise when life takes a turn for the worst.

Table of Contents

Chapter 1 7

Chapter 2 13

Chapter 3 17

Chapter 4 23

Chapter 5 29

Chapter 6 37

Chapter 7 55

Chapter 8 75

Chapter 9 89

Chapter 10 101

Chapter 11 115

Chapter 12 127

Chapter 13 135

Chapter 14 145

Chapter 15 155

Chapter 16 163

Chapter 17 179

Chapter 18 197

As little girls, Allison and Sara would dress up in their mother's clothes and wear her shoes. One day Sara pretended to dress up as if she were going to her very own wedding. She had the dress, shoes, makeup, the flowers, and she knew whom she wanted to be a part of the wedding party. Her dad Logan would walk her down the aisle. She always dreamed of having a fairy tale wedding like those she saw in magazines. These are the things that Sara would often reminisce about. Allison Ely was Sara's best friend.

Both girls grew up together in what would consider a toxic environment. They knew the love was there but sometimes would question it because her perception of love and relationships was distorted. Sara knew there had to be a better love than what she was shown. Sara and Allison eventually wanted a better life for themselves and their family. They would watch tv shows and movies, look in magazines and imagine the life and loving family they could have. The girls would often go into this make-believe world when they were younger to escape the reality of the life and environment they were in.

Sara was often told how ugly she was or that she wasn't smart, and it was never said that she was beautiful. They created make-believe friends and parents, and when things got tough, this was the world they would go to.

They had a loving family, home, and many friends who adored them. Both girls' parents were wealthy, so they did not want anything in this world. This world they created went on for a long while. As the girls began to age, they no longer went to this world. However, No one knew of this creation except the girls. They didn't tell their family, nor did they tell any of their so-called friends at school. This was strictly between them.

Now, sure both girls knew they had loving parents and knew their siblings loved them. However, it did not always feel that way. Jonathan, Sara's brother, was always being blamed for everything that went on and things that were missing. Patricia, the oldest, did what she could to take care of her siblings because their mom Sybil was always working, and dad was never around that much because he worked overnight some days. He was there but not there. Most of the time, Sara never saw him at night, and then when he got a new job, she rarely saw him because he was too much into his work.

Jamal took over the duties of looking after his sisters when Patricia and Jonathan were old enough to leave and move out. Sara and Allison's world had many things they always wanted but never imagined they could ever achieve it. The girls were so close that many thought they were twin sisters. The girls built a strong bond with each other. Sara didn't have the house she often looked at in the magazines and the family that was so well put together in the photos. Often, when they would have guests over at the house, Sara would be too embarrassed because she was always worried about what other people would think.

She grew up in a small town not far from the Taylor county line where everyone knew everyone, and she didn't come from money like Cynthia. Sometimes they would barely have money for groceries and essential things. She can remember her mother shedding tears because they didn't have food to eat. She was so worried about how she was going to feed her family.

Sybil was a praying woman, so she prayed, and it hurt Sara's heart to see her mother this way. She was just a child, so there wasn't anything that she could do. One thing she remembers is her mother praying for God to make a way and provide her family with what they needed. That day, a neighbor stopped by and bought a box of food for the family. Sybil was overjoyed, and Sara saw her eyes light up because her prayer had been answered. Sybil was happy, so this made Sara happy. Other times, they wouldn't have hot water or electricity because of hard times.

She saw the struggle that her parents and siblings had to endure and wanted to be someone who made something of herself that would earn her a lot of money to take care of her parents. She wanted to be able to buy and give them anything they wanted because they did the best they could to keep a roof over her and her siblings' heads and provide to make sure all the children graduated from high school. Yes, she thought they deserved the world. They were both very hard-working people, and she wanted to return the favor to them.

She had seen them always helping and praying for others and giving their last, but when they were in need, people quickly turned their backs on them. She thought they deserved more than that. The ones that they would pray for were the very ones that would begin to turn their backs on them and spread all kinds of lies that were not true. A lot of people that were family members always thought they were holier than thou. It wasn't because they were like this; it was just how they carried themselves and didn't act like everyone else.

Her dad was also a minister, so people always came up against him. When the very ones who betrayed him were scared with an illness or someone they knew was on their deathbed, whom would they call? Sara's dad. Her dad could have said, "No, you did this or that to me and said all kinds of things about me that were not true." Instead, he didn't bring up what they did; he simply began to pray for them. He was always thought of as a leader in the community. She really couldn't understand why this was happening. No, they were not perfect. No one is, but they strived to live a life that was pleasing to God. Sara was just amazed at how family members turned so quickly on him. She remembers one cousin who said,

Logan called her and her brothers names, but that wasn't true.

She was also the family member that was close to Sara, who would end up sleeping with her boyfriend in high school. Yes, it amazed her how the family turned on each other. A family that was close at one point. A Family that is quick to hide behind their sins yet can point fingers at everyone else. Family and friends that smile in your face, laugh, and stay at your house would be the very ones who would turn around and gossip about you and scandalize your name.

Yep, she saw the good, bad, and the ugly. Logan and Sybil were talked about and made fun of. Others hoped that their marriage would end. However, God has allowed them to be together for over 50 years. People were hoping and wishing they would get a divorce, but they never did. Their love is still going strong today. The family would always go to church every day except Saturday. However, this wasn't the case at all.

Sara and Allison would have to get their hair pressed with that hot comb! They both hated getting their hair pressed but loved the results afterward. They had a lot of family and friends who would come and visit. They would come regularly, it seemed. Some of them even sat down to eat. Logan was such a great cook. Sara loved her daddy's food. She would always sigh with relief when she got home, and he would be in the kitchen cooking a pot of beans over the hot stove. That is not to say Sybil could not cook because she could cook various things. However, Sara would often say her dad was the best cook in the world!

Chapter 2

Sara and Allison went to Corinthian Jr. Elementary ; six hundred eighty-two children attended the school. As you can imagine, it was very small, and not many people of color went there. Sara tried to fit in with the crowd but always stood out like a sore thumb. Kids would make fun of her, be mean and call her out of her name a lot. One day in class, she met Jasmine, who would become her close friend throughout elementary and high school. They attended Corinthian High school, home of the tigers. The mighty tigers!

Allison was still Sara's best friend even though she was two years older than Sara. Jasmine was the only friend that Sara invited over to her house and who she allowed to stay the night. The girls would have a blast in school and out of school. Jasmine would always do Sara's makeup and hair when it was their school's dance. She was good at that. Allison would come over and stay the night, making it even more fun. The girls talked about almost everything and loved to sing together, especially Sara and Jasmine. They would do this often in school. Sara wasn't a singer, but her friend Jasmine could hold a tune. They'd often talk about how they would change the world or what they wanted to be when they graduated from high school. Sara kept changing what she wanted to do because she wasn't sure. She did not know what her passion was at that time. The girls were now seniors and just having fun dancing, singing, and being funny. Jasmine was always the funniest person in the group.

One day, Sara noticed that Jasmine was not herself. She is usually happy and always had a smile on her face. To be honest, Jasmine looked as though she had been defeated.

"What's wrong, Jasmine?"

Sara asked.

"Oh! Nothing. Just not feeling my best."

Jasmine said. Sara responded,

"I know when something is wrong with you. What is bothering you?"

Jasmine exclaimed,

"I don't want to tell you because I think you'd be mad at me."

Jasmine thought Sara would be judgmental. However, Sara was the very opposite. She would never talk about anyone knowing how she grew up, and her parents just raised her better than that.

"What is it, Jasmine? What is going on?"

Jasmine looked at Sara with tears filling in her eyes and her head held low and said, "I am pregnant."

Sara replied, "Are you sure?"

Sara continued, "How could this happen? I mean, I know how it happens, but to you? What on earth? We had plans, and we weren't even out of high school, and neither of us talked about boys too much. We were children just having fun, so we were not boy-crazy."

Sara hugged her friend and told her it would be okay. She couldn't wait to meet her adopted baby nephew. Sara asked, "Well, have you decided on a name?"

Jasmine quickly said, "Whoa! I just found out last week. I have not been thinking about names or any of that. Well, we can think of some names soon."

Her mom was on the phone at home while cooking a pot roast.

Sara asked her mother, "Are we going to have cornbread with that, Mom?"

"Yes," Sybil said.

Sara told her mom the news about Jasmine. Sybil was shocked and in disbelief. She never expected that to happen to Jasmine so young. She told her daughter to continue to be a friend to her and be there when she needed it. Of course, she was going to continue to be her friend. That was not a reason to stop.

High school had come and gone too soon. As the girls went their separate ways, they lost contact with each other. Sara did not know exactly what she wanted to do after high school. One day, her big sister Patricia called to see if she wanted to get into this program that helped individuals get a trade. Hesitation sat in at first, but the more Sara thought about it, the more the idea did not sound like a bad one. Sara didn't have to live on campus because her sister's husband worked at the facility as a teacher. She met a lot of interesting people, and some became her friends. Her only wish was that she had kept in contact with some of them. This is not how Sara pictured her life to be. She expected to be married, have a degree, and build her dream home from the ground up. After completing her trade in Business Office Technology, she decided to go to college.

Chapter 3

ara went to college, and she lost contact with Jasmine. Sara got to experience a freedom she never had. She met guy after guy. Some she dated, and some were strictly friends. She was having fun and enjoying life. Sometimes she would miss class because she overslept, and other times because she stayed up all night hanging out with friends and drinking coffee. She and her friends loved to hang out, talk, have sleepovers and drink a lot of coffee; however, Sara's grades began to crumble, eventually leading her to academic suspension. This was when her world started to take a turn.

"How could I have allowed my grades to suffer? Sure, I missed a class here and there, but maybe that was only two or three at the most." Sara thought to herself. Nevertheless, she found herself having to write an appeal to the committee to get off academic suspension. She wrote a heartfelt letter to the committee and prayed that she would get another chance.

As she waited nervously to hear from the committee, her friend Tamia and Sharon kept her lifted in prayer. These two ladies were constantly praying for Sara and encouraging her when she needed it the most, and Sara would do the same for them. Decision day had arrived, and Sara nervously waited to hear from the committee. Her request for another chance was approved!

There was so much excitement in the atmosphere. She could not wait to tell Sharon and Tamia the good news but knew she had to wait because both ladies were in class. Sara couldn't contain herself, so she told her best friend, Allison. Allison had been in a similar situation, so she knew what Sara was going through. Allison cheered with excitement! Sara wouldn't tell her parents because she did not want them to see that she wasn't doing what she was supposed to. They would just fuss and lecture her for very long periods of time. Sara couldn't handle that.

Finally, Tamia and Sharon were done with class, and Sara told them the good news. They both leaped with joy and shouted thank Almighty God! Sara knew she had to go into next semester to do things differently, or else she would end up back where she started. One day as Sara walked to class, she noticed a young guy staring at her. He was built nicely, had the most beautiful smile, and all his teeth were straight! She looked and kept walking by. When she got to class, he was there. The more they kept going to class, the more they would become good friends. Tamia and Sharon invited me to church, and I eventually invited Bernard. He was very sweet and kind. The more the two hung out, the closer they would become and ultimately end up in a relationship. Sara started taking a turn for the worst.

On this day, he was very clingy toward her. The guy Sara was dating at the time came to visit her. When she invited him to her room, they talked like they always do, watched movies, and went to get something to eat. He whispered sweet things in her ear and told her how beautiful she was. She never expected what was about to happen to her. He raped Sara repeatedly. She told him to stop! I begged him to stop, but he didn't. She told Sharon and Tamia, and they were furious because of what happened to Sara; her best friend, Allison, was distraught.

The people she needed to be there weren't there for her and were afraid to hug her as if she had a deadly disease. They showed no care or concern but judged her for what she did or did not do. How could this have happened to her? She had heard of other girls being raped and had felt their pain, but now she is living it. She didn't know what to do or where to run. She ran to the only thing that she knew of. She ran to other men who would do the same thing and treat her as if she was below them. They would disrespect her, use her, and call her names. For the longest, she thought that was love because she had been used to abuse. She was looking for love and trying to fill a void that couldn't be filled. She knew how she wanted to be treated but kept settling for the wrong type of man.

She would think that they meant it when they told her they loved her. She would soon realize that wasn't the case. They wanted to use her and see what they could get from her. Years passed, and the man that raped her called. Sara didn't recognize the phone number and answered it. She couldn't believe that the voice on the other end was him. He talked to her as if nothing had happened and wanted to move in with her because he was getting ready to exit the military. Sara told him never to speak to her again and lose her number. She was still hurt and shocked about what had happened to her. She began to look for love in all the wrong places. They didn't care about her. They would drive 3 and 8 hours to come and see her. She was giving herself away to almost every man that told her he loved her or that she was beautiful. She was trying to fill a void that was missing, and nothing that she did would fill it. She would go on and on until she could not anymore. Sara was beginning not to care anymore, and nothing anyone said would stick with her because she didn't feel they cared. They would only say things that she wanted to hear. She hated her job and began to dislike the church she attended.

She became even more depressed, and eventually, she moved back home. She obtained employment and worked for a little while. She did not want to tell her parents that she was going through a hard time. because she knew Patricia had gone through a lot when she was pregnant. Sara reached out to the only person who would understand, her big sister. Sitting at the desk in her parents' house, Sara thought to herself, *"I'll just send Patricia an email."*

Once she submitted the email, Patricia contacted her by phone, and they talked. Patricia feared that her little sister would go through the same things she did. She and her husband came down to pick Sara up to live with them. Sara was glad they did because that was the best decision for her life. Sara began working because Patricia got Sara to help babysit with some friends from the church.

Chapter 4

Attending church with Patricia was very different for Sara. She enjoyed it for the most part. One day, Sara met a friend who was homosexual. The friend knew Sara wasn't that way because that was something she had established at the beginning. She did not judge this friend nor think any less of her. She invited her friend to church, and she agreed to come. She wanted to show her friend that she didn't have to stay the same way if she didn't want to. Sara wanted her friend to know that there was another option, and His name was Jesus. They walked into the church building, and immediately Sara could feel the judgment.

The judgment came from a very close person, and it was a bit shocking. They begin to look down on her and her friend. They assumed Sara must be that way too. The person who was being judgmental was Patricia. Why would Patricia and her best friend begin to talk about this girl? Sara didn't understand this and knew this was not what God called them to do. She was only trying to lead her friend to Christ. On their way home, Patricia and her friend Lula talked with her and began to tell her about what they saw and how it could affect her. Sara informed Patricia that she wasn't like that, and her response was,

"I should hope not."

After that day, Sara and Patricia's relationship has been strange. She felt hurt by what she and Lula were saying. The one who she admired and looked up to be the one that would begin to turn on her. She started acting funny toward Sara and Allison.

One day they saw Patricia in the grocery store, and she began to walk really fast with her cart of groceries as if she didn't know them or that they were going to beat her up for some reason. This behavior hurt both Allison and Sara. All they wanted to tell her was what Jonathan said and to call him. They couldn't understand why she was acting this way toward them, as if she and Sara were not sisters. She acted like they were strangers.

From that day on, Patricia separated herself from the family except for Jamal. She would go and visit Jamal and his family. Sara lived a little over twenty minutes away from her, and they never saw each other unless it was something for their mother. She invited Patricia and her family over to her house, but they would never show up unless Jamal or Sybil were in town. That was the only time she would see Patricia and her family. She thought it was weird. Sometimes, she would call and invite Patricia out to the movies or go to the store with her, but she was always too busy to hang out with her.

One day Allison was scrolling through social media and found a photo of Patricia hanging out with Lula and some other people. This hurt Sara's feelings because she thought to herself, how could she hang out with other people but never could make time to hang out with her own sister? She had to be okay with what was happening and try to move past it.

It was said that Patricia thought Sara and Allison hated her. I am not sure where she got this idea or who planted this seed in her head, but this is a lie from the pit of hell. Sara loves and adores her family. Sara didn't know why Patricia was acting this way. She didn't understand but had to pray and just give Patricia her space with the hope that she would come around. Some of the people that will mistreat you will be your family members.

Sometimes you have to love people from afar and leave them where they stand. Hopefully, one day, they will come around. That is what Sara had to do. Whenever her siblings needed her, she would be there or try to help them out in any way she could because that is what family does, or so she thought. Patricia even talked about the friends Sara would hang out with or who she'd bring to church.

If we are Christians, why are we talking about others and who brings who to church? Sara never really cared for Lula, to begin with, because she reminded her so much of a past friendship that Sara did not like. This was when Sara started to pull away, and Patricia would go on believing whatever Lula told her, or so it seemed this way from the outside looking in. She didn't have time to worry about that right now. It was annoying. Time went by, and Sara met someone else who would sweep her off her feet. She and the new guy really liked each other but never were able to date due to his excuses, Sara's insecurities; and the flaws she saw in him.

One night, Sara didn't get up for class and didn't go to work. She was a no-call no-show that day. She didn't understand why she was crying all the time, had a bad attitude, and didn't want to be around anyone. She stopped going to church for a long time because there was a lot of control there and the fear of hanging out with certain members because the leaders of the church led people to believe this.

An individual began to lie on Sara, who she thought was her friend. She would go to the pastors and leaders of the church and tell them all kinds of things that Sara was supposedly doing and saying. She also reached out to one of Sara's friends at the time which was Sharon, and told her lies. The two of them began to get close because of the lies that this person was sharing with her friend Sharon.

One day in service, when Sara walked in, they asked the ex-friend if it was okay if Sara sat by her as if she had done something to her. They would talk about what was discussed in private across the pulpit without saying any names. Sara got behind on her rent. She was staying in an apartment at the time. She went to look for help from the church, but they said, "We do not help when it comes to things like that (light bill, rent) because they were not that type of church."

Yet, they made sure they were well kept, driving their nice luxury cars, going to fancy restaurants and shopping sprees while staying in 5-star hotels; yet people were in need. She thought the church could help her get what she needed, but they didn't. Before she had to leave, she realized that she had not had her menstrual cycle. She thought maybe it was late due to stress. She had a gut feeling about taking a pregnancy test. The test showed up two solid pink lines, and Sara knew she was pregnant. How would she explain this to anyone?

One day, her best friend Allison knew something wasn't right. She kept observing Sara's behavior. Sara became sick and needed to go to the emergency room, and Allison went with her. When she got called back, the nurse asked if Allison could give her and Sara some privacy. That is when the nurse told Sara she was pregnant. She knew she was, but she just needed confirmation. Allison got called back in, and Sara began to cry an ugly cry like someone had just died.

Eventually, the university had to let Sara go because she was not meeting expectations. Tamia and Sharon helped her pack her things so that she could move back in with Mom and Dad. This made her even more depressed. Benjamin was there after the baby was born. He kept in contact with Sara and her parents for a while. She even took the baby to visit him and his aunt. He would make sure to call and speak with his daughter almost every day. Then, he went missing In action.

Sara never really knew what happened to him. The phone calls and visits stopped abruptly. At this point, Sara stopped caring and wanted to give up on life. She was a single parent, living from paycheck to paycheck, living on government assistance, and hopping from job to job because she didn't like her employment.

Sara pondered if life was even worth living. She thought her life was over and she was just another statistic to the world. Sara started to look for new jobs and go on interviews because she knew she had to take care of herself and her baby. She was barely getting any child support, and the support stopped coming. Things just kept happening back-to-back and seemed to go from bad to worse in her mind.

She knew Allison would always be there for her. When she wanted to give up, Allison wouldn't let her. Sara's parents were very upset with her and informed her how disappointed they were in her. Her parents did not want her to go down the path she was going. They wanted her to finish school and go on to do great things, but they never stopped loving her and being there for her.

Chapter 5

Sara met another guy after a few years and some months whom she thought was the sweetest guy she had ever met. Although he was very heavy set, she could look past that because the weight can always be lost. They talked all the time on the phone and sometimes talked so much that they both would fall asleep. The two often spent a lot of time with each other. Not too long after dating, he took Sara to a football game where she had no idea that she would meet his family for the first time. After the game, they went to have dinner, and he ordered her food. However, when it was time for them to get ready to go, Sara asked for a to-go-box. The guy's father did not appreciate her not eating all her food. He looked at Sara with an impertinent look and then whispered something to his wife. This should have been Sara's red flag moment. However, she did not think it was a big deal. She just kept thinking about the mean look he gave her. She thought to herself, *"This man does not like me."*

She should have run away, but she wanted to see where the relationship would go. Everything was going great, she thought to herself. Each time she went to visit her boyfriend, he would always be on his computer playing video games. She was left by herself out in the living room, eating and watching movies often.

One day, her co-worker informed her that her husband had a friend that they would like her to meet. They just wanted Sara to be happy and know what she was going through.

Sara's friend Ashley asked, "Is it okay for me to give him your number?"

Sara responded, "Sure, it's fine. Give him my number."

This was not normal for her to be left alone while in the same house so he could play games. She is dating a guy, and all he wants to do is play games and leave her by herself. What guy asks someone to come over and then leaves them while he goes play on the computer? The other guy and Sara started to talk over the phone to get to know each other. They talked about meeting up. However, this was not the case. She informed him that she was in a relationship with someone, so she would not be able to do that. He got upset and never talked to Sara again!

In the back of her mind, she wondered how that relationship would've turned out. One night she forgot her phone in the bathroom, and it was unlocked. Her boyfriend found it and read the texts where the guy and Sara had been talking, and then he accused her of cheating on him. He assumed that she met up with this guy and that they had a relationship. The guy and Sara never met up.

All Sara's boyfriend kept asking was, "Why did you do it?"

She had not done anything, in her opinion but talked to a guy who showed interest in her. Sara's boyfriend had all her stuff by the door because he was done. He expected her to continue to come over, sleep, eat, and watch movies by herself, though. This should have been red flag number two. She should have just kept going and never looked back. Unfortunately, she did not do this.

Sara chased what she thought she wanted because he was a sweetheart, only to find out he was a mean person. She later learned that she was pregnant with her second child. This is when things started to sink even more. The person he was and always was started to come out. This man treated Sara like trash! This is red flag number three.

No man or woman should treat another human being as if they are scum beneath their feet. Sara cannot excuse the toxic behavior of this man. However, she knew that she was talking with someone on the phone but never did she meet him. There was a part of her that wished she had gone through with it because maybe he would have treated her better than this guy had. When she told her boyfriend she was pregnant, he immediately became very upset and started going off on her. He believed it was the other guy's baby and not his. He and Sara stopped talking for a while. He did not want to tell his family about her being pregnant.

He told her it was because she did not have a college degree and they were not married. He knew his family would not approve of this relationship. Honestly, he just kept lying and could not remember the first lie he told, so the lies always switched up. He had no intentions of telling his family because of the image he wanted to portray to them. Sara gave him an ultimatum. She told him either tell them by December 31st, or she would tell them. He chose not to tell them. On Christmas Eve, she picked up the phone and left a voicemail for the family. Sara's message said,

"I am your son's friend. I am pregnant with his child. He has no intention of telling you all, so I am calling to tell you. I would love for you all to be a part of this baby's life. If you have any questions, then you can call me."

He informed her that his mom had called him and asked him if there was anything he wanted to tell her. He was mad at Sara for a long time. His dad had stopped talking to him because he was disappointed. Nevertheless her parents were upset, but they did not stop talking to her.

Months went by, and he would show up to some of her doctor appointments which were very few in between. She was left to go by herself or sometimes with her friend Allison. His mom eventually called Sara and told her she had a lot of baby stuff for her. She also informed her that she did not want to bring it because it was heavy, and she didn't want her to have to carry it upstairs. His mother was lying about all of that. She was just waiting until a DNA test proved that her son Christopher was the biological father of the child.

Sara couldn't wrap her head around why these people were treating her like scum, and his parents raised their daughter's son as if his mother had given birth to him.

He still calls his grandparents mom and dad, but they have the nerve to judge Sara. It is all about image to them. They always acted as if they were too good for others even though they had skeletons in their closet. She would get into heated arguments with the mom and sister because they believed all the lies their son would tell them.

Sara dealt with this while she was pregnant. His mom, brother, sister, and dad did not like Sara at all. They really tried hard to pretend as if they just loved her so. As time went on, Sara stopped reaching out to her then-boyfriend. She kept ignoring all his phone calls from him and emails. She didn't want to continue to have fights with his family.

His brother made it seem as if Sara was a whore and slept around with other men as to why he didn't think it was his brother's baby. He knew nothing about her other than what his older brother had told him. This family judged Sara instead of taking the time to get to know her.

The one that gave her the hardest time was his mother. She was cold as ice when it came to Sara. There were so many altercations between them and Sara that if she did not get things off her chest, she would explode on all of them! She kept trying to prove she was worthy despite everything her boyfriend told them. They didn't like her, and the feeling was very mutual. Christopher wanted Sara to abort the baby because he didn't want to have that responsibility on him. He wanted them to think that he was this great guy, that he was living a life for Christ, and that he did no wrong.

Sara asked him, "Why would you want me to abort another man's baby? If you don't think you are the father of this child, why would you request me to do that?"

She was furious and began to yell at him. She never liked him to see her cry. This is the same guy who told Sara that he loved her only six months into their relationship. She never thought he would act a complete fool when she told him she was pregnant with his child. He accused her of purposely getting pregnant. The person close to Sara asked her if she got pregnant on purpose. She was in utter shock!

Sara responded in disbelief, "No, I didn't do this on purpose. I took the necessary steps needed."

His family never reached out to Sara to see how she was doing. It was perfectly fine because they didn't know her, nor did they know if this was their son's baby. Sara was very depressed at this stage in her life. She had already gone through something traumatic, and now she is dealing with Christopher and his foolishness. She should have known this was too good to be true. He was putting on an act with her. The moment she told him she was pregnant, his true feelings came out. Sara said to herself, *"How could I be such an idiot? How could I have allowed this to happen?"*

She thought he was different from all the other guys, but he was literally the same as all the others she had dated. She felt like she messed up again. She seemed to just keep messing up. Time passed, and Sara gave birth to another beautiful baby girl named Joy.

Chapter 6

She lived in an apartment with her baby girls. It was small, but it was very nice. Sara never liked clutter, so she kept everything simple. She would enjoy movie night by herself and spending time with her babies. One thing for sure, when the babies got older, they knew they would be loved because Sara made sure of that. She didn't want to allow her girls to grow up in a toxic environment. Sara, Autumn, and Joy loved going to the park and the grocery store. One day while at the store doing some grocery shopping, she met a man who was tall, built, and had a bald head. She glanced at him but turned away quickly because she didn't want him to notice that she was staring at him. She needed to get some ice cream down the aisle he was on. She didn't want to go down the aisle because it would be awkward for her. Nevertheless, she went anyway.

As she passed him, he said, "Your perfume smells good."

Sara couldn't look him in the eye because she felt embarrassed, but she thanked him and continued to get the ice cream. Her daughter talked loudly because she wanted popsicles and kept saying, "Popsicles, Mommy! Popsicles!"

Sara got the ice cream and the popsicles and kept moving right along with the other groceries they needed. As she was pushing her cart with baby Joy and Autumn in it, she got the feeling that someone was following her. So, she pulled her cart over to the aisle where the butter was to allow the person to walk past. Instead, it was this same man who told her the perfume smelled good following her.

She said, "Excuse me, did you forget something? Or need anything?"

He said, "As a matter of fact, I do. May I have your name?"

Sara paused for a moment and replied, "My name? Why?"

The man politely said, "I would like to know who I am speaking with. Plus, I cannot allow you to get out of this store, not know your name, or ask if you're dating anyone."

Sara was stunned by his forwardness but graciously said, "Well, my name is Sara, and I am not looking for a relationship right now. I am just focused on my daughters and myself now."

With a hurtful look in his eyes, he said, "I understand, and my name is Ruben."

Sara extended her hand to shake his and said, "Well, it is very nice to meet you, Ruben."

He kept smiling at Autumn and Joy and talking in baby talk to Joy, and then he and Autumn began to play peek-a-boo.

"I hate to break up the party, but we really must be on our way," Sara said as she started to push her cart away. Ruben said,

"Excuse me, Sara. Please take my business card and call me when you are free. I would love to learn more about you, Joy, and Autumn."

Sara took the card and said, "Thanks! I will keep this in mind."

The two departed and continued shopping. When she, Autumn, and Joy were done, she knew they would be hungry. Sara said with a loving voice to her daughters, "Mommy does not feel like cooking. Do you want McDonald's?"

Autumn excitedly said, "YES, Mommy!"

When they arrived at the house, she got a text message from Allison, who wanted to come over. Sara responded by saying "Yes," and asking if she would be able to watch Autumn and Joy while she got the groceries out of the car.

Allison texted her back, "Sure."

When Sara finished with the groceries and putting them up, she told Allison all about their adventure in the supermarket. Allison asked Sara to tell her all the details. Sara said,

"Umm, there is not much to tell, really. He is a nice-looking man, and although I saw him from across the aisle, I knew I could not just have anyone around my child."

As Sara was informing Allison about the man, Allison told Sara, "Just to be careful because although he may be nice, he really may not be a good person."

It was Thursday morning, and Sara had to get up early to drop Autumn and Joy off at daycare because she had an interview with Brown and Chance Mortgage Realty because they were looking for an administrative assistant. Her interview was a 9:00 am, so she knew she had time to stop at her favorite coffee place Pink's and pick up her order. Sara was a regular there, so they knew what kind of coffee she liked and always had it hot and fresh for her. All she had to do was call them and tell them she was on her way. When she went to go and pick it up, they began to question her.

The workers said, "Oh my god, Senorita! Where you headed?"

Eduardo and Gustavo were always a handful, and they liked to be nosy. Sara laughed and said, "I am off to an interview if you must know."

She wore a black pants suit with gold trim, and her hair was up in a beautiful professional bun with gold earrings and low heels. "God bless you on your interview and safe travels,"

They said as they handed her coffee and pastry. Eduardo and Gustavo always threw an extra pastry in the bag for her and Autumn. Sara often wondered why the two never got in trouble for this. She loved how nice they were to her, Autumn, and Joy. As she was on her way, Eduardo called her and wanted her to tell them how the interview went and to take her and the babies out to eat because he had something to tell her. Sara, Gustavo, and Eduardo were friends and would occasionally go out to eat with she and her children. Sara arrived at her interview and met Mr. Brown and

Mr. Chance. Mr. Chance said, "Hello Sara, we are so glad you made it safely."

The interview lasted for an hour and thirty minutes because they really enjoyed talking to Sara, and Sara really enjoyed their conversation. They would let her know their decision on Monday around 12:00 pm noon.

"Thank you; it has been a pleasure speaking with you both today."

Sara stopped at her favorite clothing place, Mel's house, to see what new outfits she had. Mel was very fond of Sara, Joy, and Autumn because she thought of them as her own children. Mel did not have children, and after several rounds of IVF, it failed at every attempt, so she took Sara, Joy, and Autumn under her wing. When Sara first stopped by, she and Mel talked for a very long time about many things, and Mel sometimes would even look after Autumn and Joy. She has always told Sara not to hesitate to stop by because she would be the first to know about any specials and new items she received. She also gave Sara the "Mel's House" discount. Sara did not worry about having to pay for a single thing.

She and Mel often took road trips with Autumn and Joy and went to conferences because Mel knew where Sara came from and saw greatness in her. She knew when Sara wanted to give up, but she never stopped checking on her or allowing her to visit or sometimes stay the night. She wasn't going to allow Sara to give up on herself, nor was she giving up on her. After Sara finished shopping, she went by the daycare to pick up Autumn and Joy. When Autumn saw Sara, she ran over to her and gave her the biggest hug. She remembered Eduardo and Gustavo wanted to take them out for dinner and talk to Sara about something. This was odd because they never really talked to her about anything Sara thought. Meanwhile, she was back at the apartment getting Autumn and Joy ready. Eduardo told Sara to dress nice, but one thing about Sara was that she was always going to make sure she looked good, even on her worst days. She never likes to leave the house looking a hot mess.

She met up with Eduardo and Gustavo at Delia's Delights, a very fancy Italian restaurant, and she ordered Autumn spaghetti, and Mel had stuffed lobster ravioli in a wine cream sauce, a salad, and water with lemon.

Eduardo said, "Well, we wanted to bring you here because we need to tell you something. Remember when you came into Pinky's, and we always knew what coffee you liked, and we always threw in pastries for you and Autumn?"

"Yes," Sara said with hesitation in her voice.

Gustavo interrupted Eduardo and said, "What Eduardo is trying to say is that he and I own Pinky's."

Sara said with a very loud voice, "Oh my god!"

Gustavo said to Sara, "Shh. Please keep your voice down, or they will kick us out."

Sara always wondered why they never got in trouble for giving her pastries with every cup of coffee. Eduardo said, "There is something else we must tell you too."

"What is it? Is it good news?" Sara asked.

Gustavo told Sara, "You no longer must pay for anything in Pinky's. We don't want your money anymore. Also, should anything happen to either of us, you are the beneficiary of our insurance and Will. We also want to leave Pinky's to you and Autumn, and Joy. Should you have any more children, which you are, then we will continue to add and adjust."

Sara began to cry hysterically and could not stop for a while. The news of Mel and now Pinky's was just exciting and overwhelming that they wanted to help her and her children so much. Sara thanked Eduardo and Gustavo and told them words can't describe how happy she was and thankful for what they had done for her.

"I don't deserve all of this," Sara said with tears in her eyes and a trembling voice. Both men shouted,

"You deserve that and much more, Sara! You are a beautiful, kind, sweet, loving young lady and we love you. We also would like you to go back to school and finish."

Sara explained, "I really can't right now, you guys. I mean, I have taken so much time off, and I have two babies now and I am trying to find a job that I enjoy going to."

Eduardo stopped Sara and said, "Just go back to school, Sara. I am not saying you must go back this instant, but please go back. You are too smart not to go, have so many great ideas, and are very organized. I don't know what school or job wouldn't want you. If they don't want you, that is their loss because they don't know what they are missing."

Sara humbly said, "That means the world to me. Both of you mean the world to me."

They hugged each other once they got outside and told each other they loved each other. That Monday, Sara had to return back to work after a long and very exciting weekend. She got up and got ready to head to work. She was a customer service representative for a call center, and she hated that job. She wanted to get out. It was going on at 3:30 pm, and Sara needed to get off work at 4:00 pm because she needed to go and get Autumn and Joy.

Her phone began to ring, and she didn't recognize the number. She thought to herself, "If it's important, they can leave a voicemail."

They didn't leave a voicemail and kept calling her back. Sara was annoyed because whoever it was kept calling her. This last time, they left a voicemail. It was from Brown and Chance Mortgage company. Sara thought that maybe they were calling to tell her she didn't get the job. She battled with low self-esteem and never looked at herself as beautiful or worthy. She was rejected many times until she thought that rejection was her life. She couldn't understand why Mel, Eduardo, and Gustavo would take a chance on her. Maybe they see something in her that she doesn't see in herself. Sara did not want to call them back and hear, "We really liked you, and you were our top pick. However, we went with someone who was more qualified for the job."

She mustered up the courage to call them back.

"Hello, Sara! This is Mr. Chance with Brown and Chance Mortgage Company. How are you?"

"I am doing well," Sara said.

Mr. Chance said, "I was calling to find out when you can start working for us."

"Excuse me. You mean you are hiring me for the job?" Sara said.

Mr. Chance chuckled and said, "Yes, Sara, we would be fools not to! We love your personality, your charm, you have a sweet spirit, and we just thought you would be the best fit for the job."

"Thank you so much!" Sara said with excitement.

She told Mr. Chance that she would need to inform her current supervisor because she would need to put in her two weeks' notice. Sara was filled with joy, but again she kept doubting and questioning herself. Sara wondered in her mind why are people being so nice to her. Perhaps, it is that little girl from Sara's past who was mistreated and talked about. She was often called ugly, dumb, and stupid. Because she was told this since she was a little girl, she thought maybe that's who she was. She just couldn't see herself thriving, beautiful, and more than enough. Things seemed to be going Sara's way for a while. The man she ran into the supermarket that day he just so happens to see her in the post office dropping off a package.

The gentleman spoke to Sara, and she immediately recognized him and spoke back. Ruben asked Sara out to dinner and this time she agreed to meet him at a restaurant. Their date was set for that

Friday evening. Ruben left the post office with a smile on his face. Sara had butterflies in her stomach after agreeing to have dinner with this man. Not only was Ruben a nice-looking man, but he was a very sweet man too.

Who could Sara call to watch Autumn? I mean, she did have choices because everyone seemed to love Autumn and Joy. She also knew that Autumn loved her Godmother, Allison. Allison is a free spirit and loves to take a walk on the wild side at times. She knew it would be a miracle if she could get her to watch Autumn and Joy. She reached out to Allison, and Allison shouted of course, she could watch the babies. The day had come and Sara was getting ready for her Friday night date. As she was getting ready, she heard Professor Klump from the movie Nutty Professor in her head. Friday night at 8:00 got me a date, I cannot be late, and that will be so great! Sara laughed at herself. She loved just being home watching movies and having fun. Sara got into her car and headed to Stacy's Diner, where Ruben was waiting for her. He pulled the chair out for Sara to sit down and pushed it back in.

"Oh, what a gentleman," Sara said.

Ruben responded by saying, "Well, is there any other way to be?"

Sara smiled. They received their menus, and everything looked good Sara had a hard time deciding. As usual, she ended up getting a veggie burger, French fries, and a milkshake.

Ruben said, "We are at a diner, and you order a veggie burger."

Sara said to Ruben, "What is wrong with that? I do not always eat meat. Sometimes, I just want some good ole veggies."

Ruben said gently, "I hear you."

Sara and Ruben began to talk almost all night. The diner was a 24-hour diner. Sara told Ruben that it was getting late and that she needed to pick her daughters up from the babysitter. Ruben asked Sara if she couldn't stay for a little longer and have ice cream. Sara reminded him that she had a milkshake with her meal. He shook his head yes and offered to get ice cream again soon. Sara told Ruben that she would like that. Sara thanked Ruben for a wonderful evening and how much she appreciated it. She explained that she hadn't been out in a while, and it was nice to have a good evening and great conversation. She felt herself getting tired and starting to ramble. So, she cut the conversation short and stood up to leave. Sara really liked him, but she had a feeling that something seemed off about him. Although he was a nice guy she got a feeling that something was up with him. She and Ruben would begin to hangout often and started to get close to one another. One day while they were walking in the park, Ruben asked when he could meet her daughters. Sara started feeling comfortable enough to allow Ruben to meet her daughters. So, they made plans for the weekend to hang out, and Sara would bring the girls with her.

Eduardo and Gustavo were starting to get worried about Sara, Joy, and Autumn because they would see less of her, and she hadn't been coming in to get her usual coffee. Eduardo decided to call Sara and check on her. When Sara heard Eduardo's voice, she got excited and screamed,

"EDUARDO! How are you, buddy?"

Eduardo responded with happiness,

"I am doing well. It is very good to hear your voice. Listen, Gustavo and I have been getting a little worried about you. Are you and the babies doing, okay?" Sara answered,

"Yes, we are doing well."

Gustavo jumped on the phone, and said,

"Sara, it's a guy, isn't it? You haven't been coming into the shop as much, and we barely hear from you now, so I know it's a guy. Spill it, Sara!"

Sara explained that she in fact, met someone. She told them that he was a very nice man and he loved her and wanted to meet Autumn and Joy. He is very handsome. "

I knew it! What else could be keeping our Sara away from us?" Eduardo said.

Sara began to tell them all about Ruben. Sara got off the phone with Eduardo and Gustavo because she was meeting Mel for lunch at her shop. During lunch time, Mel would close her shop up just so she and Sara could have privacy and not be disturbed while they ate. Every time Mel saw Sara, she would pray with her. Mel could tell something was off. Sara told her all about Ruben. Mel warned Sara to be careful. Mel was very adamant about Sara introducing her children to Ruben. She kept telling her something just didn't seem right about him, and she had an uneasy feeling about this Ruben guy. Sara felt like Mel wasn't giving him a chance and she hadn't even met him yet. It was the day for Ruben to meet Autumn and Joy at the park. He was just as exciting as Sara was. They arrived at the park and as soon as Sara introduced them Autumn and Joy gave Ruben a big hug! This made Ruben feel special because he didn't have any children of his own. He and Autumn and Joy had so much fun as if they knew each other already. He would run and chase the girls and push them on the swing and catch the girls when they came down the slide. Sara was happy to see that her daughters was happy. It had been ten months already and Ruben had already started having strong feelings for Sara; and wanted to take it to the next level. Ruben began to tell Sara how he felt for her and that he loved her very much. The only thing that came out of Sara's mouth was her questioning him about it being so soon. She questioned him about him saying he loved her and he responded by saying,

"Is that so bad for me to love you?"

Sara answered and said,

"I mean it seems a bit fast and we are still getting to know each other."

Ruben told Sara that he had strong feelings for her. Sara wasn't ready to say something she really didn't mean. Sara loved him in a Christian way, but not in the sense of in a relationship type of way. Sara said to Ruben,

"Umm, I thought we were getting to know each other. Hold up, why are you getting upset because I didn't say I love you? Like, who does that?"

Ruben said, "I just thought because we were hanging out more and I finally got to meet Autumn and Joy that we were moving in the right direction."

Sara chimed in and said, "Yes, we are but again, we are still getting to know each other, and I don't think we have to move too fast."

Ruben was a big time Executive for a Fortune 500 Company and was working his way to become the next billionaire in the Black Billionaires magazine edition because they are always listing the richest people and interviewing them of how they started to where they are now. Sara was pretty sure Ruben was used to always getting his way. This didn't sit well with Sara, and she remembered that her friends and Allison told her to be careful. She ignored the early signs that were in Ruben and took the relationship to the next level. This time Ruben wanted Sara, Autumn, and Joy to move in with him. Sara had her own place and loved the peace and quiet and she didn't want to have to uproot Autumn and Joy and deal with anyone's bad attitude. Ruben had this charm and was very good at convincing people to do what he wanted them to do. He had all these good ideas and presented them in such a beautiful package, that you would just end up saying yes.

Three months later, Sara, Joy, and Autumn ended up moving in with Ruben. The first few months were great! They talked about boundaries and many more other things. Autumn and Joy had their own room which was very large. They lived out by the lake which had a spectacular view overlooking the city. The house had five bedrooms and five bathrooms. It also had a swimming pool that was gated for safety and Sara loved that.

One morning Sara was cooking breakfast and Ruben walked down and asked her where his coffee was. That didn't sit well with Sara because Ruben wasn't rude or mean to her before. Why would he act differently now? Sara made his coffee just the way he liked it with a shot of espresso, caramel drizzle, and milk. He gave her a kiss on the cheek before heading out the door. Sara made her coffee and got Autumn ready to head to daycare while she went to work. Mel, Eduardo and Gustavo knew that Sara moved in with Ruben and they thought that was a very bad idea. They even offered to get Sara somewhere to stay but she just wanted to do her own thing because she thought she knew everything. One night Ruben and Sara began to argue with each other over Sara's job and taking Autumn and Joy out of the Little Preschoolers Day care center because he thought the girls should go to a top notch, dignitary school. Later that night, Sara told Ruben that she would take her daughters out of the preschool they were currently attending to enroll in the more state of the art one and she would also end up quitting her job because Ruben didn't want her to work.

Ruben thanked Sara and told her he could tell she haven't experienced the finer things in life, but now she, Autumn and Joy will get to. Sara didn't care about materialistic stuff because she wasn't that type of woman. Ruben started to become a little more controlling every day, but Sara thought it was just a phase and that he was acting this way because something happened at work, so she let it go. He told Sara that his parents were in town and wanted to meet her. He did not give her any heads up he just told her. Sara questioned Ruben and asked,

"Why would you just now tell me this? I could have gotten the house cleaned and my hair done; and been better prepared for their arrival. Will they be staying the night?"

"No. They just want to come and meet the love of my life."

Ruben said.

"They should be here by 8:00pm and we will eat dinner at the house with a hired chef, so you will not have to clean, cook, or any of that, okay?"

"Okay, but next time can you let me know in advance?"

Sara said politely. He didn't answer her and told her to make sure that she puts on something nice. He didn't want to give his parents the wrong impression of Sara. Sara felt some type of way about Ruben. He said it with an attitude, " Please go get ready and dress Autumn and Joy in something nice. I don't like the clothes that you buy for them. They look cheap."

Sara was stunned by what Ruben said. She responded,

"Why are you being mean Ruben? Are you going to pay for their clothes?"

Ruben stopped and said,

"Sara, you have my black card which has unlimited spending so please take it and get you some new clothes too. Sara what is with you? Every time someone says something nice or tries to do something nice to you, you always question it as if you're not worthy or good enough."

Chapter 7

Sara admitted that she is trying not to let her past still haunt her from when she grew up. Maybe Sara was stuck in the past and just couldn't see her way out. The men she had dated never treated her like this, so this was much different for her. She was used to verbal, mental, and emotional abuse by the men she dated. Ruben was being extra nice and rude at the same time, so this behavior confused Sara. Nevertheless, she proceeded to do as he said and went and got new clothes. She found her a very elegant purple dress, and Autumn and Joy had a matching one. It was nothing revealing because she didn't like showing her arms or legs because she didn't like the way they looked. She knew she needed to work out and get in shape, so she made sure to buy things that covered her up.

Once she got back home, Ruben was there waiting for her and wanted to know what took her so long and demanded that she go get dressed before his parents arrived. The chef was already in the kitchen starting to prepare dinner. It was a very beautiful layout. They had tulips, Lily's, wine glasses with gold-trimmed plates and gold silverware laid on the table, and each guest had a placement card. Sara didn't understand why he had place cards on the table.

Sara asked, "Ruben, why do we have more than five place settings? Are there others coming to eat?"

He answered, "Yes, my siblings and aunts and a few cousins. I hope that's okay."

Sara looked very disappointed and overwhelmed because she hadn't planned for all the guest to be at the house. The doorbell rang, and the guest finally arrived. They loved on Sara, Joy, and Autumn and were very nice to them. Sara heard one of his relatives and sibling say that he did a good job. Sara smiled and pretended that she didn't hear that. When she went up to hug Mrs. Mulberry, she didn't get quite the welcome like the rest of the family. This woman didn't hug Sara back and she looked her up and down as to see if the woman her son chose was good enough for him. She was very distant to Sara and wasn't very fond of Autumn. The whole time at dinner she was asking Sara about her educational background, where she lived, and asked her about the kind of work she does. Sara began to ignore some of the questions because the night was just getting more overwhelming for her, and she needed to go give Autumn and Joy a bath and put them to bed.

"Hold on before you go honey," Ruben said.

He begins to hit his fork on his glass and began to make a toast. After the toast was over, he kneeled on one knee and took Sara's hand and asked her to be his wife. With such shock and joy Sara leaped into his arms and said yes, I will marry you!

The family began clapping loudly and whistling and rooting for the both of them. The whole time he was planning an engagement dinner and wanted to keep it a secret from Sara because she always had to know what was going on. She was hoping that his mom would loosen up and be excited, but she wasn't. She sat at the table with her lips poked out and rolled her eyes. His dad just smiled and told his son Congratulations.

What was going on with Lady Mulberry? She seemed very disappointed in her son's decision to marry a woman who was not up to her standards or Rubens. Ruben went and hugged his mother and she whispered something in his ear, but Sara just knew it wasn't anything good.

After dinner, everyone sat in the dining room to talk and get to know each other better and the chef brought some dessert and coffee after everyone had finished their meal.

Ruben's mother asked Sara, "So, Sara tell me, what do your parents do?"

Sara said, "Well my mom works for an accounting firm and my dad is a lawyer."

Then, his sister asked, "Where did you grow up?" Sara responded that she grew up in a very small country town right outside of the Taylor County line.

The sister continued to talk, "You must miss home, don't you? I mean you went from a country town to living in the big city, that is quite a change, isn't it?"

Sara answered, "Yes, but I am getting used to it and I have met some wonderful people."

The sister kept grilling Sara with questions. She wishes Allison was there with her because she wouldn't take too kindly of how they were treating Sara and would have gotten smart with Lady Mulberry and Layla his sister.

There was something about Layla and Mrs. Mulberry that Sara didn't like. All night long the two kept staring at her and Mrs. Mulberry kept making mean faces towards her. It used to always be Ruben and his sister hanging out and now he will have a wife and children that he will spend all his time with exclaimed Layla. Ruben told his sister that he's sure she will be alright, and he will still make time for her and the family. He is very big on that.

Once everyone was done with dessert, they went into the living room area to relax and wine down. They put on a movie and enjoyed popcorn. However, Sara could feel eyes on her. She happened to turn around and his dad was just staring at her smiling and making her very uncomfortable. She was getting very tired, so she thanked everyone for coming and wished them all a goodnight. Just as she was walking away Lady Mulberry thought she whispered but Sara heard her say, "She is wishing and thanking everyone a goodnight, and this is my son's house! Who does she think she is?"

In shock, Sara just continued to walk to the bedroom to lie down. The next day, she received a phone call from Gustavo. Gustavo told Sara that they were worried about her. Sara advised them that they are doing very well and Ruben is good to them. Sometimes, Ruben says things that make Sara question him. She thinks that it's all because he's stressed about work. Gustavo asked if she was ok and that Ruben if abusing her. She told him that he wasn't abusing her. No one seems to like Ruben. Gustavo told Sara if she needed anything to please reach out to him and Eduardo because they would be there in a heartbeat.

Back over at the house, Sara and Ruben discussed the dinner.

"Listen, I know my mother can be a handful, but she means well."

Ruben said. Sara said with an attitude,

"Is that what you call it? Your mother and sister snarled their noses at me, and your mom kept looking at me rolling her eyes and saying sly comments. I think that's more than being a handful. I get the impression she doesn't like me."

This woman did not like Sara or Autumn. She thought Sara was stupid and didn't care for Autumn because of who her mother was. She seems to love Joy for some reason. Maybe that was because Joy was the baby. Sara could not understand why she treated Autumn one way and Joy another way. You would think this wouldn't matter, since she had a baby out of wedlock and her daughter had a child so very young. Now, how can they treat someone like this and then walk around like she is all high mighty? Or that there are no skeletons in her closet. It's like she feels comfortable with turning her nose up at others because of who they are and where they come from. Mrs. Mulberry is such a hypocrite.

Oh yes, Sara learned of this information from someone who knew Mrs. Mulberry quite well. They didn't get along too much either. She was always making trouble everywhere that she went. She always acted like she knew everything and hated to be wrong. You could tell this woman the sky is blue, and she would say, no it's not blue. That is just the type of vibe Sara got when around this woman. Sara felt like she was a narcissistic woman. She wasn't helping it by the rude looks, whispers, and a snarl on her face all the time. Sara sometimes wondered who raised this woman to be like this. Or did something happen in her lifetime that made her turn this way. She really could be a nice and sweet lady if she wanted to. She just chooses to be mean and hateful to Sara all the time because she doesn't like her.

At this age, she should know better than to treat anyone so disrespectful. Do you think she cared? No! Do you think that she would apologize for her behavior? No! She would come and bring stuff or handout things but wouldn't give anything to Sara. She would do this right in front of her.

Sara didn't care as long as she didn't do that to her girls. Mrs. Mulberry is mean! The only time she would try to be nice is when one of her children or her husband would tell her how to be. Sara didn't understand why you needed to tell a grown more mature adult woman how to be. They should know how to behave! She never told Sara that she was sorry for her behavior. Instead, she just kept being her usual self as if nothing happened. She walked around like her behavior was excusable because she thought she was in charge and everyone she comes in contact with must do what she says. One of her ways of apologizing was to just tell stories from the bible and then buy you a gift or food and she really thought that was alright to do.

This type of behavior would soon rub off on Ruben. What makes matters worse is she's supposedly a Christian woman and to act like that, that is not acceptable! She didn't like the fact that Sara had different beliefs than her son. She would always try to get her to join her church and come into agreement with her ways and beliefs. Mrs. Mulberry didn't think that anyone could be saved or would go to heaven unless they were under a certain organization/church that she was in. Sara couldn't believe that this woman was spewing that type of mess on people and some people actually believed her, until they got to know God for themselves and found out that this was a lie. She even went as far as to get the children on her side and conform to her ways. Ruben said,

"My mom is over the children's ministry in church, she serves her community well, and she works with the children in the church too. She's a pillar to her community and I find it hard to believe that she and my sister did or said anything to you."

Sara knew this was Ruben's mother talking, but she acted like Sara was full of the devil. The way Mrs. Mulberry acted as if she was dating Ruben. She just didn't like the fact that Ruben found someone he wanted to spend his life with. Anyone that she thought tried to come in between them, she didn't like or if anything was said about that person, she didn't like them. She didn't want to get to know anyone but rather just believe the lies.

This woman almost got into a fight with someone. She wanted her grandchild to go with her back to the farm and visit family. Her oldest grandchild didn't want to go. She then turned to the child's mother and said, "All it takes is a look."

The mother said, "What look? I didn't give anyone a look. If your grandchild doesn't want to go, then she doesn't have to go."

One of the youngest grandchildren started to cry. He was just a baby. His dad was holding him and as the mother was going out the door, Mrs. Mulberry decided that she would hold onto her grandchild and began to pull on her arm trying to get her from her mother. Her son was just standing there trying to get the children to go with him. The mother then says,

"You better let go of my child."

She moves Mrs. Mulberry's hand from her. She didn't know how she managed to get her children and put them in the car. When she was trying to get away the children's father, he knocks the keys out of her hands and they went underneath the car. She pulled on his shirt to pull him back and got the keys.

The mother began to yell at Mrs. Mulberry and said, "You just stand there and watch him do this? You are just standing there and not even saying anything."

Mrs. Mulberry said, "I don't want to get involved."

I mean Mrs. Mulberry and her son were coming up against the child's mother all because her children didn't want to go with her. There was no court order set in place that they had to go. They just didn't want to go because they knew she was mean and especially to the oldest. The mother looks over into the car and all she sees is her babies crying because they watched all this foolishness take place. It was just an awful thing to hear how a mother and son teamed up to come up against the children's mother based off an assumption.

She told the child's mother that she wasn't going to bankrupt her son and that her son could do whatever he wanted to do, as if giving him free range or will to do whatever he wanted to do with the baby's mother. That is ridiculous! I don't understand how someone can be that cruel to a person and never know them but only goes by what has been brought to their attention. You don't take time to get to know them for yourself? You just listen to all the negative words and then act accordingly? WOW! The whole thing is absurd. Sara didn't understand why he thought his mom was such a sweet loving, Christian lady who was a pillar in her community.

Well, maybe she didn't know them as well as she thought she did. Being frustrated, Sara said, "I am not going to argue with you. I am going to excuse myself and go to bed."

As she was walking away Ruben said, "Yeah go get in the bed I paid for."

Sara rolled her eyes. Before she got into bed, she showered, brushed her teeth, and said her prayers.

When Sara woke up the next morning, Ruben was nowhere to be found. She tried calling him because they usually have breakfast together with Autumn and Joy every morning. This morning, Ruben wasn't there. She kept calling him and texting him, but there was no answer. She messaged him, saying, "Where are you, Ruben?"

He normally tells Sara his whereabouts so neither of them would worry about the other. For him to not answer or pick up his phone is weird to Sara. She was concerned that something bad happened to him. How could she live with herself because they just had an argument the night before? Sara begins to pray that Ruben would come home safely. It was 1:30 in the afternoon, and Ruben came through the door with pink box of doughnuts in his hand and a cup of coffee.

"Where were you?" Sara asked.

Ruben answered, "I was out getting breakfast for my three favorite people."

Sara told Ruben, "No, you didn't stay here last night and you're just now getting home. It's almost 2:00 in the afternoon."

Ruben angrily said, "Who are you to question me, Sara? You're not my mom."

Sara said, "You're right, I am not your mom, but I am the woman you so happen to be madly in love with and the woman you want to marry or is that all a lie."

Ruben answered, "Yes, that is true. I just needed time to calm down and I put my phone on silence. I left the house and went for a run and then went to get breakfast and didn't realize how late it was getting. Please forgive me."

Sara felt bad and said, "Of course, I forgive you but, in the future, please make sure your phone is on at least vibrate."

"Will do!" Ruben said.

"Where are you, Joy and Autumn headed off to?"

"We are going to go meet up with my friends that I haven't seen in a while. I am not sure how long we will be out or if we may stay over with Allison or Mel. I will call or text you and let you know."

"No!" Shouted Ruben. "You will not be staying at anyone's house. You and the girls need to come back here tonight. If you are not here, then I will go find you both."

"Is that a threat? It's okay for you to go out and stay all night and not show up until this afternoon, but Lord forbid I do it? That is not right!"

"Why are you shouting in front Autumn and Joy? Please forgive me Sara, I have a lot going on right now and I do not mean to take it out on you."

"I forgive but please do not do this again."

Autumn, Joy and Sara got into the car, and she put the girls into their car seat, and drove down to Elpaso to go and visit Eduardo and Gustavo. To her surprise when she got to the house Allison and Mel were waiting for them on the couch. They both jumped up and ran to both Sara and the girls.

"Oh, my goodness!!! I cannot believe you are here. What are you doing here?"

"We wanted to surprise you both."

Autumn really missed them both and hugged both and didn't let go for a while. "You haven't really been in contact with us, and we just wanted to see you and make sure you are doing okay Allison said."

"Yes, I am doing fine. Is this an intervention?"

"No, this is not an intervention, this is just friends getting together who love each other and care about each other's wellbeing."

"Oh, okay," said Sara.

"Now, that we are here, what are we going to do?"

"Well, we have a fun filled weekend ahead of us."

"Umm. I wish I could stay the weekend, but Ruben wants me and the girls to come back tonight."

"Are you insane?"

Gustavo said.

"You cannot go back tonight because it is going to be very late. Why do you put up with this guy?"

Mel asked.

"He seems very controlling."

"No, No. He is not really. He's just concerned about Autumn and Joy."

"If you say so."

Allison said. Allison was one who was always going to speak her mind no matter who was around. Allison said,

"That's okay y'all are here. Here is what we will do. We will just take a trip to Abbeville, TX and spend our time with Sara, Joy, Autumn there. Does that sound reasonable to you Sara?"

"Yes, that will be fine, and then you all can finally meet Ruben because I am sure you will like him. You must get to know him. Let me give him a call and let him know that we will be having a guest."

Sara went off into the guest bedroom and called Ruben while the others were in the kitchen making something to eat and taking care of Autumn and Joy.

"Hi honey, we will be back tonight, but how do you feel about having guests over Saturday and Sunday?"

"Who is it?" Said Ruben.

"It's my friends that have been wanting to meet you. I think it's only fair because you didn't tell me about your family coming until the last minute."

"I suppose that will be fine. Where will they be staying while in town?"

"At our house, of course?"

"You mean my house?"

Ruben said. "Please do not start this with me. I have asked you not to say such things. You wanted me to up and move and quit my job, so I would like to think of it as my residence now too. I expect you to be nice because they are nice people and will read you like a book."

"Oh, please! I am not worried about your little friends."

"My little friends? They are grown men and women, so watch your mouth!"

Sara hung up the call abruptly. Once Sara finished her call she headed down to the kitchen.

"Okay, that settles it. You all are coming to Abbeville and you are staying with me at the house. That is only if you want to. You most certainly don't have to, but I would love for you all to be there."

"Yes, whatever makes it easier on you, Sara. If you want us to stay, then we will stay," Mel said.

They rejoined each other in the living room that night, where they played games and sang songs, and listened to their favorite gospel artist. Before they all retired to bed, they joined hands and said prayers. Allison led the prayer. She and Mel are such prayer warriors and they always kept Sara, Joy, and Autumn in prayer. The next morning everyone got up early and made breakfast before heading out on the road. Eduardo and Gustavo rode together and Allison and Mel rode with Autumn, Joy and Sara. They finally pulled up to the nice big lake house and Allison could not believe her eyes. They all wanted to know what kind of work Ruben was into. They told Sara the house was simply breathtaking and beautiful.

"Thank you, I am sure Ruben would love to hear you say that."

Sara smiled. When they got into the home Ruben was there waiting to meet them.

"Hello, I am Ruben. I have heard so much about all of you. Sara just couldn't stop talking about you. I was like, when will she be quiet? We get it you like him."

"I suppose Sara told you that she and I are engaged to be married?"

"Yes, she told us all, and we plan on being at the wedding."

"If there is one," mumbled Gustavo. They went to the kitchen where the chef was preparing everyone's favorite. "Wow! You have a chef too?"

Yes, I try to ease the load on Sara."

"Hmm, that is mighty kind of you whispered Allison."

Once dinner was done, everyone changed into their pajamas and went to the theater room, where they would watch at least two movies that night. We all joked and laughed, and Sara just looked around the room and smiled because this is what home felt like to her. She had missed her friends when she moved away from Simpleton, GA, a few months ago. The later it became Sara reminded everyone that they had a big day ahead of them.

"We will eat breakfast in the morning, and then we will head out, and I will show you all around Abbeville, and then we will do some shopping, and you will pick out your bridesmaid dress Allison and Mel"

"We will help," Eduardo said, "Because you know we love fashion."

"Yes, I know. Goodnight!"

Once Ruben thought everyone was asleep, he began to fuss at Sara, and one point, they got loud.

"Please keep your voice down! You don't want to wake the whole house."

Sara could not sleep because Ruben just fussed at her and then cussed her out because he really didn't want them at his house.

"You better watch your tone with me, and on May 28, 2005, they will all be family, *your* family too, so you might as well get used to it."

The next day, they rose and walked downstairs to the main dining area, where they would be served breakfast. "Good morning, everyone!"

"Good morning, sweetie pie," they all said.

"How did everyone sleep?"

"We slept all right. I cannot complain," Allison said.

"How are you doing this morning, Sara? You look tired."

"Yes, I am a little tired, but I will be okay. Ruben and I were up pretty much all night talking. Alright, let's finish breakfast and get our day started."

They finished their breakfast, got dressed, and headed to town. They stopped at mostly all the bridal shops they could find, but Sara just could not find the dress she was looking for. Allison and Mel didn't like any of the dresses either. Those two ladies laughed and made fun of some of them because most of the dresses looked hideous. Mel said,

"Sara, yes. I hope it is no trouble, but may you please make my wedding dress?"

"I would be delighted, Sara. I thought you'd never ask."

"What?"

"You wanted to make my dress?"

"Yes, but I wasn't going to say anything, but it's all about what you want. I hope you don't mind, Allison and I were talking about the dresses, and I plan on making our bridesmaid dresses too."

"Oh, that will be wonderful. I know whatever you make is going to be fabulous!"

"Whew! I am so glad you are going to make the dresses, Mel."

Gustavo said. These little shops did not have anything that I would have approved any of you ladies to be in. They all laughed and headed down to Dukes Tasty Barbeque joint. It was a small hole-in-the-wall type place, but the food there was amazing. Sara loved to eat their brisket, mac and cheese, and baked beans. The potato salad wasn't bad either, and for dessert, they had the most delicious peach cobbler. Sometimes Sara would drive into town to pick up an order of it because it was just that good. Ruben hated when she would pick up food orders because they had a chef to cook all their food, but sometimes the food wasn't all that great. He could have just had an off day, but Sara was really craving Duke's peach cobbler most of the time.

Some nights she would sneak off and run to town and sit and eat at the restaurant. There was pure silence at the table at the restaurant. Sara looked up and saw Allison tapping her foot, Mel was rocking back and forth, and Eduardo and Gustavo kept saying, "My God, because it was just that good."

Once everyone was done eating, they all decided that they were tired and wanted to go back to the lake house and take a nap. Once they finished their naps, they decided to go to the park and walk around the pond because it was very peaceful. Ruben did not want to go, so he stayed behind and watched Autumn.

"Are you happy?" Allison asked.

"Am I happy? Ugh yes. I am okay. I just have to get used to this lifestyle because you all know it's not where I came from. This is all very new to me."

"We just want you to be happy. If you ever need anything, please say something."

Back at the lake house, Ruben was outside in the sunroom where he was grilling steaks, burgers, veggie burgers, corn on the cob, veggie kabobs and the list goes on. Sara was surprised to see him grilling.

"Hello, said Sara. What made you grill? I didn't think you could stand my friends."

"Well, I figured you all would be extremely hungry after a day out on the town."

"Yes, we are starving! Where is Autumn and Joy, by the way?"

"Oh, they are asleep. How were they?"

"The girls were very good, and we played, and I took them outside and let them run and jump until they tired themselves out."

"Sounds like you all had a blast."

"Yes, we did. The girls are very lovely children, and I adore them."

"Okay, well, I am going to go and get changed, and I will be back to help you."

"If you don't mind, I'd like to see if Eduardo and Gustavo would like to come and talk about men's stuff while you and the ladies stay inside and make sides for the meat. Is that okay with you?" Ruben asked.

"Yes, I will let them know." Sara went back into the house and told her friends what Ruben suggested or wanted.

"Oh, we don't have a problem with that."

As Sara watched from the kitchen, the men seemed to be having a wonderful time, and it looked as if Eduardo and Gustavo were giving Ruben tips about grilling.

The food was finally done, and we sat down to eat. Sunday morning arrived, and it was time to say our goodbyes. We knew this was the hard part even though we didn't live far from each other. We always hated to say goodbye.

"Thank you for having us over. We are going to miss you."

"I will miss you more."

Sara walked them to the door and outside, and they gave each other a big hug. As they got in their car she didn't go in until they pulled out of the driveway and got down the road. It was back to being in a huge quiet home.

"Did you enjoy your time with your friends?"
Ruben asked.

"Yes, we had such a wonderful time. I missed them dearly, so I was glad to see them. Also, Mel is going to make my wedding dress and her and Allison's bridesmaid dresses."

"Wow! That sounds good. How much is she charging? She isn't charging me anything, but I cannot allow her to do this for free. I know she thinks of me as her daughter, but it wouldn't be fair."

"Well, let me know a fair price, and I will have it taken care of."

"Thanks! I think I'll go and lay down now because I am extremely exhausted from this weekend."

While she went to take her nap, Ruben had other things in mind. He would barely pay Sara any attention. He was always on his phone discussing business. Often more times than not, Sara, Joy, and Autumn were left at the house by themselves. She often wondered what kept him so busy. Again, she knew something was off, but she continued to ignore the signs because she knew that deep down inside, he was a sweet, caring, and loving man, and she could overlook him fussing at her or his sly comments.

Chapter 8

It was the spring of 2005, and Sara only had two weeks before the wedding day. Everything was going as planned. They planned to have a huge wedding with 250 guests. She had everything ready from food, venue, and where people would be sitting. By this time, Autumn had turned eight years old. And Joy turned 5. How time flies by! Both girls would also be a part of the wedding party.

"Well, I have to go and get my last fitting before the big day. Autumn, we are going to drive to ElPaso and we will stop by Pinky's to get coffee and, of course, see Eduardo and Gustavo."

"I'd like that."

Autumn said. Off they drove to go and see her friends. Once she parked, she and Autumn got out of the car and opened the door to Pinky's Eduardo ran and gave both a big hug. He was so excited to see them.

"What brings you to this side of town?"

"Well, if you must know, we drove to see you and Gustavo, and I have to go Mel's to get fitted for my dress."

"You're really getting married, huh?"

"Yes, Ruben has flaws, but it will be alright."

"We all have flaws, don't we?"

"Where is Gustavo?"

"He went to run an errand, and I know he would love to see you."

"Yes, I would love to see him. If I am not able to then I will message him. Hopefully, we all can get together before the wedding. I see that your customers are coming in like a flood, so Autumn and I will take our drink and pastry to go. Love you." Sara said.

"Love you both too!"

As they both walked to their car, Eduardo's eyes began to fill with tears, but Sara did not know why he almost cried.

"I guess he just misses me," she said.

They had just had a loving and fun weekend. Maybe they felt Sara was making a mistake, but neither of them could get through to her because she was going to do what she wanted to do. Back at Mel's, Sara tried on her wedding gown for the big day.

"It looks very fabulous on you." Mel said.

"This is the most beautiful dress I have ever seen," said Sara. "You really worked hard on this."

"Yes, because you are like my daughter." She knew what Sara liked and didn't like.

She then pulled out Autumn's dress, and it was very beautiful and pink, just like Joy's. Sara loved pink, so her wedding would include pink and grey colors. Before leaving, she and Mel sat down to talk while Autumn played on her phone and was entertained by the tv and other things that Mel had at her shop for her.

"You are going to be the most beautiful bride I have ever seen."

"Thank you, Mel. I have always pictured how I wanted my wedding ever since I was a little girl, and it's starting to happen."

"Are you sure you want to get married? Are you positive?"

"Yes, you know Eduardo asked me the same thing."

"I just want to make sure you are happy."

"I am happy with Ruben."

"Okay, if you're happy, then I'm happy."

The girls thanked Mel and headed back to Abbeville to their lake house. Ruben was not at home when they arrived, but he did leave Sara a note.

The note read: I will be in late this evening. I hope to see you soon. Please let the chef make you anything that you want. Love you, Ruben.

After Sara read the note, she put it in her nightstand. She always kept the notes Ruben wrote her. She wondered why he kept having these late nights. He must be working on a project. Sara knew that's why he had been fussing lately because he was stressed about this huge project. If he got the deal, then he would become a partner at his company.

Once Sara, Joy, and Autumn got washed up, they had the chef make them a delicious yet simple meal. Meanwhile, back at Rubens's office, he got on the phone and called Sara to let her know that he had to work late again. Sara thought that maybe he was seeing someone at this point. He had left the house and had more than one late night at the office, but that thought quickly went away.

Ruben finally arrived the next morning, which was the day of the ceremony. He told Sara that he loved her and couldn't wait for her to become Mrs. Mulberry. He got what he needed and headed to the venue to get freshened up because the venue had everything they needed. Many of the guests were able to stay inside what looked to be a beautiful mansion, and that is where the ceremony would take place. Sara had a car service the day of the wedding for her and the girls, so the driver drove them to the mansion to get ready for the big day.

However, Sara also requested a car service for her friends and family. She couldn't have a car service for her and not her family. Mel and Allison got ready and helped calm Sara's nerves. She would nervously peek out the window and the door to see all the guests that would arrive that day. She made sure her parents and siblings were well taken care of and could not wait for her dad to walk her down the aisle. Mommy Sybil would be escorted by both Jamal and Jonathan. Sara put on her dress, designed specifically for her by Mel. It did not have a veil, as Sara didn't like or want anything covering her face. It was a beautiful long beige dress embroidered with sparkling beads on the train of the dress, and she had a tiara with bling that would match the wedding dress.

She looked amazingly beautiful that day. The guest were still arriving. Finally, the doors of the venue closed at 1:45 pm. The ceremony was set to begin at 2:00 pm. As the makeup artist and hairstylist were putting on the final touches, Autumn and Joy came over to give their mom a big hug and kiss and told her she looked very pretty. Sara's hair was done, and makeup finished. She just needed to put on her shoes and get her bouquet of flowers which were pink lilies, white lilies, and a mix of green Chrysanthemums. As the door began to open, out would come Autumn, Mel, and Allison with their gorgeous attire.

Sara's dad saw her and told her she looked very beautiful and gave her a kiss on her cheek. As they walked down the aisle, the song, "After All is said and done," was playing, and the attendees arose from their seats as the bride made her way to her soon-to-be husband.

Ruben was in awe, and Eduardo and Gustavo had such a gleam of joy in their eyes because Sara looked so beautiful. The pastor said a few words, and the vows were read, the rings were put on, and the couple said, I do. Ruben kissed his bride, and the crowd cheered with joy. Well, some of them cheered and clapped. Ruben's mother and sister were not particularly happy. They had a slight smile on their face, not because they were happy but because they could not believe Ruben would marry a woman like Sara. She was no good for him, and they didn't like the fact that she had two children who didn't belong to Ruben.

These two women would plot and plan of how they could make Sara's life miserable to the point she would have no choice but to divorce Ruben, so the woman his mom wanted him to marry could come right along and snatch him before he could find anyone else. This is just how wicked that woman can be. She wouldn't stop until she tried to make Sara's life a living disaster. At the reception hall, guests were seated at their assigned tables where they would have a five-course meal and dessert. The dance floor was lit up in pink with Mr. and Mrs. Mulberry. The lovely couple walked in with the DJ announcing them, and they all screamed and clapped for the newlyweds. The two had their first dance, and soon it was time to cut the six-tier cake.

As they danced, Sara looked at Ruben, and he looked at her as if no one else was in the room. The night was late, and the two left as they had to catch a flight because they would honeymoon in Scotland. Before they left, Autumn and Joy came to give their mom a hug and told her they would miss her.

It was a night full of fun, excitement, and all the festivities and food you could imagine. The newlyweds were enjoying their seven-day and seven-night stay in Scotland. They often posted pictures of the fun they were having. The last night of their trip, Ruben received a phone call.

"Who could be calling you while we are on our honeymoon?" Sara asked.

"Oh, it's my job."

"Are you serious? We are supposed to be enjoying our time, and your phone is supposed to be blocked from having any work calls. What is so important that they couldn't wait until we got back."

"I have to try and win this client over in order to become a partner, and the guy they left in charge is not doing such a good job, and they think we will lose him, so we will need to change our flight to head back really early in the morning."

"What?" Shouted Sara.

"On our last day here? Is work more important?" Ruben began to yell at Sara.

"I must work so that you can keep up with your fancy lifestyle."

"My fancy lifestyle? I wasn't fancy when you met me, so that's a lie. I'm not a materialistic girl," shouted Sara!

Ruben informed Sara to calm down so they wouldn't get kicked out of the hotel.

"This is supposed to be the happiest time of my life, and you ruined it by bringing up work and taking phone calls from them. They have no boundaries and no respect!"

"I know you're upset, but trust me, this is going to be good for us. I just need to take care of this business, and then you and I can spend all the time we want together and go where we want. We can take Autumn and Joy out if you'd like."

"That sounds good and all, but I am still very upset."

Sara's ears began to turn red because she was very upset with Ruben. The next morning, the two got up very early to head to the airport. They would arrive back in the United States around 10:00 am. When they arrived, it was silence from the airport to the lake house. The two barely spoke to each other the whole plane and car ride back.

"Let me get your bags," said Ruben.

"No! I can get my own bags, and I don't need your help. Shouldn't you be going? You don't want to miss your meeting or client, right?"

"Can we not do this?"

"I'm not doing anything!"

"Look, I don't have time for this. I have to shower and get going. I should be home by 6:30 pm tonight. I can have the chef fix us a really good meal."

Sara completely ignored him and walked off into the couple's bedroom and slammed the door. Ruben did not check to see if Sara was okay. He grabbed his jacket and rushed out the door. Sara did some shopping in the small city because she wanted to change the furniture and make it to more of her liking. She loved a home that was cozy and comfortable. The lake house was not either of those things. She wanted to hire painters too. She discussed her ideas with Ruben, but he didn't want her to really change anything in the home. A lot of the items in the house were given to him by his mother. He and his mother were close. A little bit too close that others would question the relationship. Anything he asked Sara, he made sure to ask his mom and dad to see if it was a good idea too. He would share his ideas with Sara but never listened to anything she told him. He would then come back and tell Sara what his mother said, although she had told him the same thing, to begin with. Why was he like this? She noticed their relationship early on but never paid any attention to it that much. Whatever this woman planted into his head, she had her hooks in him very strong. She did notice how he would never really take her side, even though his mother would be in the wrong, and that was a bit strange to her, especially when the Bible says in, Matthew 19:5-6, *For this cause shall a man leave his Father and mother and cleave to his wife: and their Twain shall be one flesh?*

Sara was starting to notice that Ruben was not cleaving to her. His mother was calling the shots, and Ruben was the puppet on the string. She wanted to get Ruben's take on the color scheme and changing out the furniture when he got home – that's if he came home for the night. She began to walk around every room of the house and take a vivid picture of how she'd like each room to be decorated and what paint colors to add. Each room should be inviting with warmth. She couldn't wait to tell Ruben about her plans to make it feel more like home. She stayed up all night waiting for Ruben to get home. However, he didn't show up all night. She called and texted him, but there was no answer. She waited a few minutes and then tried the line again but still no answer.

"Here we go again," she thought. "Why does he keep doing this to me? This is so frustrating and annoying. Just pick up the phone," she said to herself.

Finally, she'd give it another go, and he answered.

"Why didn't you answer your phone?" Sara asked.

"Oh, I wasn't in my office. Me and the guys went out to eat and talk."

"That's all you have to say for yourself? Me and the guys went out and that is why I stayed out late?"

"Really? Do you not want to be married? Or maybe just not married to me? You've been staying out all night as if you have no family, Ruben."

"Look, I will be home shortly. Is everything okay at the house?" said Ruben.

"Yes, I just wanted to go over some color schemes and get your input about changing up the furniture in the home."

"Yeah, we will definitely have to talk about it because some of the stuff my mom gave me, and I don't want to get rid of it."

Sara rolled her eyes and told Ruben that she'd talk with him later. Later that day, when Ruben got home, he was too tired to talk about anything and wanted to just shower and go to sleep.

"Can we talk about the furniture and paint after I get up?"

"Yea, that will be fine," she said.

"Also, my mom is coming into town for a few days."

"Okay, when?"

"She will be in tomorrow. May you call the maid service so that they can come to clean the house?"

"Sure," said Sara.

She got up and started to think hard about why Ruben wanted to stay out all night and how his mother was coming into town, but Sara knew his mom did not like her and let alone stand Autumn. Maybe it was because Autumn and Joy were not his, or maybe she felt like Sara had taken her place. Nevertheless, Sara began to make the phone call to the maids to come and clean the home. She usually liked to clean things herself, but Ruben always insisted that she call maids.

Back in El Paso, Eduardo and Gustavo were busy working on their next adventure. The two wanted to get into real estate, buy homes and flip them, and purchase commercial property and rent it out to consumers. These two brothers were doing quite well for themselves and always stayed busy but made sure they were never too busy for Sara and the girls. Mel was busy making custom dresses for her clients, so she had not seen Sara and Allison. She stayed busy with work and travel. She has always wanted to travel, even though she wasn't traveling a lot; she was beginning to get out there and explore more. It was Saturday morning, and the maids had come to clean the house. By the afternoon, they were done. The doorbell rang just as they were heading out a few minutes later.

"Whom could that be?" wondered Sara. She knew it wasn't her friends because they were busy and knew to call her before coming over. She opened the door, and to her surprise, it was Ruben's mother.

"Hello! How are you?" Sara hugged her even though she knew his mom didn't want her to. The lady just looked at her and leaned as if trying to push Sara away.

"I am fine." She never did hug Sara back. She wasn't hiding the fact that she didn't like Ruben's wife and Sara had no idea what she did to deserve this behavior.

"Ruben is just getting up, so I am sure he will be out here soon. Can I get you anything to drink?"

"I know where the kitchen is, and I can help myself she said."

Sara had a long pause and said, "Okay."

His mother asked, "Are you in college, or are you finished?"

"I was in college, but I am not anymore."

"Oh," she said with a snarled voice and a frown.

"How long do you think Ruben will be?"

"I can go check."

His mother responded, "I will go and knock on the door. I am his mother, he will answer me."

By this time, Sara was fuming on the inside because this woman had come into their home, and she was rude more than ever. She just needed to calm down. She took a deep breath, but it wasn't helping, so she decided to call Allison because she always seemed to know the right things to say most of the time but sometimes, she wanted to choose violence over peace, and she knew she was busy, so she decided to call Mel who had wisdom beyond her years. Just as she was going to step outside, she heard Ruben calling for her.

"Yes, I am here. Where did you go?"

"I am outside and was going to make a phone call. Can that wait because my mom is here?"

"Sure."

She was boiling on the inside because he wanted her to stop what she was doing. It was okay if he was on the phone or if he'd stayed out all night. She shouldn't question where he was, but he felt the need to question her, she thought to herself. Ruben went and got his mom's bag out of her vehicle and carried them to the guest room she'd be sleeping in.

"How are your parents his mom asked?"

"They are doing well."

It's not like she cared. She doesn't even like her parents.

"I will try and have them come down for a weekend so that I can show them around."

"I think they'd like that."

"Oh, okay."

Sara rolled her eyes and walked off. She came back, and his mom continued to ask her questions.

"Have you and Ruben talked about having children?"

"No!" Sara exclaimed. "I am not ready for any more. Autumn and Joy are enough right now."

"Autumn is very tall."

"Yes, that she is."

"Ruben probably shouldn't have any. He just has to find the right woman," His mother said.

"Excuse me? Don't you think he has found the right woman? I am sorry you feel that way. Not only has he found me, but he married me too. I guess you will have to deal with that."

She just looked Sara up and down and walked away.

Chapter 9

A few years later, Autumn was twelve, and Joy was nine years old and having fun visiting their grandparents and playing with their cousins. Autumn and Joy, and their cousins always loved having a cousin sleepover. The girls talked about any and everything and usually would stay up all night planning the next prank!

Mrs. Mulberry was visiting again. She once again talked to Sara about children and wanted to know when she and Ruben would have some.

"Well, he and I have not brought up children, so I think we are good there. I am sure when that time comes, we will discuss it."

Why is she asking Sara about children? Why would she want Ruben to have children with her when she knows she doesn't like her? Ruben interrupted Sara's conversation in her head to talk about a play that was showing this weekend. He knew Sara loved plays, but also his mother loved them too. Mrs. Mulberry seemed to criticize everything that Sara said, wore, and did. She could not seem to do anything right. Her behavior towards Sara and her daughters, especially Autumn, was beginning to get worse and worse.

All she would ever do was talk about Ruben's brother and his wife and how well off they were. How they had beautiful children, and she graduated college. She did this to rub it in Sara's face, but one thing about Sara, she never disrespected his mom because she was raised not to treat anyone with such disrespect, and she knew her Mother, Sybil, and her father would not tolerate it.

She had to listen to his mom boast about her daughter-in-law and their kids, while always looking down on Sara and itching for something to say negative against her. It didn't help that Ruben would tell her everything. All Mrs. Mulberry did was go back and repeat to others in her camp who she was close to what was said about Sara. Yet, she called herself a Christian and is full of love. More like full of hate!

"Please, God, let this woman be leaving my home soon," Sara said to herself.

"I am not sure how Ruben is not aware of this. Maybe he is, and he chooses to ignore it. I will talk to him about her behavior once she leaves because I don't want to ruin their time here Sara said to herself."

"The play was so moving, touching, and inspiring," Sara told Ruben.

He just smiled and turned to his mom. "What do you think, mom?"

"It was nice." She said.

As they were walking to the vehicle, Ruben got a phone call.

"Who was that?" Sara asked.

"It was my sister and my brother. They want to come down and visit too."

"Oh, how lovely. When will they be coming?"

"Tomorrow."

"Okay, I will be sure to have everything together when they arrive."

Sara took a deep breath. It is so weird how she was just thinking about them, and now they are coming.

"Lord, give me strength."

She said.

Of course, Mrs. Mulberry was excited! She didn't waste an opportunity to throw things in my face. She knows that once the sister-in-law comes, she will be ignored as if she were invisible. They made it to the lake house, and Sara said her prayers before she went to sleep. Ruben usually never prayed with Sara and hardly ever prayed for her. She woke up and thanked God for allowing her to see another day. This was the day Ruben's brother and sister, along with their spouses, came to visit. She went into the kitchen to speak to the chef so that he could begin preparing a huge spread for breakfast because they would be at the house within two hours. Sara had just enough time to go and pick up Autumn and Joy from my parent's house because they would be so excited that their cousins would be coming to town. They hardly got to see them with everyone's busy schedule.

On Sara's way to pick them up, she decided to call Allison because she usually called her to vent all the time. However, Sara had forgotten that Allison was out traveling right now. She is doing so well for herself. She knew she could call Mel because she was full of wisdom, and she would know the right words to say and to get me to calm down.

"Hello, Mel."

"Hi, Sara! How are you doing? I have not heard from you since you got back from your honeymoon. How did it go?"

"Everything went great!"

The thing about Mel is she knew when Sara wasn't being truthful. She had known Sara for so many years and thought of her as her daughter.

"What happened?"

Sara begins to tell Mel everything. She also told her about Mrs. Mulberry, who didn't seem to like her.

"I don't know why she doesn't like me."

"Well, sometimes people do not like you and don't know why. It is nothing that you have done to them; Other times, it is because conversations happen when you are not around, and that person may have painted an ugly picture about you. Instead of getting to know you, they would rather believe the lies."

"That's not fair to me Sara shouted as tears rolled down her face. I think that Ruben was saying things about me that just aren't true, and maybe that is why his mom is mean to me."

"Yes, I do believe he did, Sara."

Before the two got off the phone, Mel began to pray with Sara and the children and told her she loved her. On the way back to the house, Autumn, Joy, and Sara decided to stop at their only favorite coffee shop, Pinky's plus; the two wanted to see Eduardo and Gustavo.

"Hello, my favorite people."

Sara said. With such excitement in the air, the two brothers ran over to Sara and the girls and gave them the biggest hugs. Gustavo asked his employee if he could make the two their favorite coffee and Joy a strawberry smoothie with whip cream because everyone there knew about Sara and Autumn. They began to get to know Joy too, and what she liked. Joy wasn't into drinking coffee like Autumn and Sara, plus Sara felt that she was too young too.

"I have not seen much of you, sweetie."

Eduardo said.

"How was your trip?"

"The trip was wonderful."

"What are you going to do today they both said?"

"I have visitors coming."

"His mother?"

"Yes, she is at the house, but also the brother and sister are coming into town today too, so I cannot stay long and chat."

"Oh gosh! Are you okay?"

"Yes, I will be fine."

"You know to call us if anything happens, right?"

"Yes, I will be sure to call you two. Love you!"

The two walked out the door to their car and drove back to the lake house to get ready for their company to arrive. Once they arrived at the lake house, they had less than an hour to get ready. Sara walked into the couple's bedroom to get ready. The door opened, and it was Ruben. From the look he had on his face, Sara knew it wasn't going to be good.

"What took you so long to get back?"

"Let me see, I went to pick up Autumn and Joy, and I stopped to see some friends and pick up some coffee, as you can see."

"I think you should make new friends and leave them alone because I don't think they are good influences on you!"

"Really."

Sara thought to herself.

"Let me get this straight; you want me to stop being friends with people I have known forever and who led me towards Jesus Christ and not away from him? You must be out of your mind if you think I am going to do that!"

"If you do not stop hanging around them, I will stop giving you money and cut you off my credit cards."

"Really? Is this some type of joke?"

"No!"

"Well, I guess you can cut me off then!"

What Sara was seeing was "like mother like son." She started to notice that Ruben was beginning to be controlling, and his mother loved to control things too. She always had to control and be the center of attention. She is now finding out that Ruben is acting like her now. She had her hooks on this boy, and whatever mom says is what goes for him, no matter if he's married. Mrs. Mulberry doesn't care about the wife, but you better listen to whatever your mom says, not your wife. Yeah, she was training him and had trained him well.

Ruben couldn't seem to break free, nor did he seem like he wanted to. It bothered him that he was in the middle, but other times it didn't seem like he cared because he was going to take his mom's side no matter if his wife was right. Sara washed her face and put on a smile because she heard the doorbell. It was Ruben's sister Layla. She gave Sara a hug. Autumn and Joy were waiting patiently for their cousins to arrive. Sara saw both of the girls looking out the window every so often.

Finally, the doorbell rang again, and their cousins Sapphire and Rose came in. The girls screamed with excitement and went off upstairs.

"Girls, we are going to have breakfast soon, so please come back down here," Sara shouted for them to hear.

"Here we go," Sara said in her mind when they were at the table eating. Mrs. Mulberry was getting started, and Sara was being ignored like always. Layla saw her brother's kids and Joy and called them beautiful, but she never said anything about Autumn. She didn't even mention Autumn or speak to her when she came in. The three ladies were having a conversation that Sara was not included in. It amazes her that when the mother and daughter get together, they feel they have to run off outside or have these side conversations about Sara. It never failed when they came around; the two of them left to go outside to take care of their plants or to act as if something outside had really gotten their attention. Oh, please! I know the game, Sara thought to herself. Sara sat at the table and talked with the children.

They usually like talking to her because she is easy to talk to. Once we were done with breakfast, everyone went into the family room to talk about life and what activities we would do for the remainder of their stay. I pulled my phone out and began to look at my social media pages when I noticed a text from Autumn, and she wanted me to come into her room to talk about something. I quietly slipped out and followed Autumn.

"Do you think I am pretty, mom?"

"What? You are beautiful and smart, Autumn. Why don't you think you're pretty? Did someone say something?"

"No, I just noticed how Aunt Layla never tells me that I am beautiful, but she tells Sapphire, Joy, and Rose all the time in front of me."

"Oh, sweetie, I am sorry. It doesn't matter what anyone says, it only matters what God says, and you are fearfully and wonderfully made. Did you know that you were made in the likeness and image of God? Yes, you are, and you are beautiful."

Autumn smiled big with her beautiful smile and big, pretty brown eyes and hugged her mom.

"Okay, I will go back downstairs with my cousins."

Sara sat on the bed to digest what her daughter had told her. Her heart was broken over the news she had just been given. She didn't want her daughter to have low self-esteem, she thought to herself. She went into her daughter's bathroom, turned on the water, and locked the door so no one could hear her cry. When she finished, she washed her face, took a deep breath, and went back downstairs.

None of them could ever pick up on what was happening with Sara. They sat there and acted as if they did not care. They never knew that she was crying because, for one, Sara never allowed them to see, and two, they never paid any attention to her. Sara kept talking as if nothing had happened.

"Why was the sister being so rude? It's bad enough that Mrs. Mulberry was there and wants to tear me apart, but now the sister wants to come for my daughter?"

"Everything okay?" Ruben asked.

"Yes, I just needed to help Autumn with something," She said.

Then, Ruben went back to talk to his family. The ladies were going to go and get their nails done. Sara decided to stay back, take care of some things around the house, and watch the little girls. The men left to get food for the cookout they were having later that evening. The girls were having so much fun while playing in the pool. Sara told them after that they could roast marshmallows by the fire pit out back. She wanted this to be a cookout to remember, so I gathered pillows and blankets, and chairs for everyone and set up a projector for us to watch movies. Everyone arrived back from their outings. They would then come out back to get the food started on the grill. Mrs. Mulberry looked around and noticed what Sara did with the backyard. Ruben's brother's wife was amazed at how beautiful the backyard looked and how Sara took time setting up everything, and she thanked her for it. However, Mrs. Mulberry looked and said, "You have been busy?"

"It would appear so," Sara answered. Ruben's sister just said, good job Sara. Sara thanked her and walked away. Before she went into the house, she told the girls that it was time to get out of the pool and for them to go shower and get ready to eat dinner. Things were going well that night, and everyone was getting along and playing games and enjoying the food the men had cooked. It was Rubens' family last night there, and they would return home the next day. The girls hugged each other bye and even cried because they were not ready to leave each other. Sara hugged everyone, and the mom looked at her as she always did and did not hug Sara back. "Why does she keep doing this to me?" Sara thought.

Once the company left, Sara informed Ruben that she needed to speak with him. She spoke to Ruben and let him know what was going on. She even expressed to him how hurtful this was to her and her daughter. However, Ruben seemed to act as if it was no big deal and began to justify the behavior his family was doing. He did not act concerned about what happened to Autumn. This upset Sara. How could he allow his family to continue to mistreat her and her child?

Since Ruben was not going to act on it, then Sara had to address her concerns to the family when she saw them in person again. She informed Ruben that she would do this, but he did not believe her. The behavior went on, and Ruben never addressed it. He kept trying to justify their behavior and make Sara believe they weren't acting how she said they were and that it was her making up stuff.

Chapter 10

One day, Layla wanted the girls to visit and have fun with her. Sara got her moment to confront the family. She informed them of their behavior and told them that this had to stop. It was clear that Ruben was talking badly about Sara, and they had a perception of her in their mind and never did get to know her.

The family did not like her based on lies and treated her and her daughter based on such things. There were so many altercations between them, and if she did not get this off her chest, then she would explode. This type of behavior went on for years. She wanted them to get to know her, not her tainted picture. She tried and tried, but nothing she said or did seem to work. She would send emails and text messages and apologize for things she did not even do or say. One day, she was advised that they all sit down and have a heart-to-heart; however, nothing she said or did would make a difference. They were going to look at her and treat her like Ruben described.

Sara was very hurt and sad because she could not understand how the so-called Christians would treat her and her daughters like scum, trash, or rubbish beneath them. Mrs. Mulberry went as far as to call Sara a stupid girl. She told Ruben this, but he did not want to hear and yelled and fussed at Sara for telling him. She never understood why he did this when she told him how his family treated her. Over the next several months, Ruben would show his behavior. She thought he was a very nice person, but what she went through with him she never imagined would happen to her. He began to abuse Sara verbally, emotionally, and mentally. He began to control her a lot more. She would need things, but he wouldn't get them for her or told her that she would have to do something for him for her to get what she, Joy, and Autumn needed. He treated her like a lady of the night instead of his wife.

One day, Sara needed to go to the store to get a few things, but when she went to get into her car, she noticed the keys were not there. Ruben took the keys and locked the door to the vehicle so that Sara could not drive the car. This was one of his ways of punishing her when he didn't get what he wanted. He threw temper tantrums often. You're 39 and still acting like a little kid. This seemed to happen often. One day she began to look for vehicles. From the beginning, Ruben told her that the car he purchased was for her and the girls, but she was starting to see that this was a lie. Another time, he cut off the internet so that she could not use it, and he knew that she had some projects that she needed to work on, but he didn't care. It didn't stop there. He went as far as to cut off the electricity to the house because he was furious at Sara. Autumn came out of her room that night and said, "Mom, it is hot!"

Sara went to the garage and flipped the breaker to restore power to the house, and Ruben went out and turned it back off. He didn't care that Autumn, Joy, or Sara was hot or that she had to get up early and get the girls ready for school. It was Ruben's way or no way! One thing he knew he could control her with was money. She had to call a cab to come get her so she could go and get what she needed but when she went to go and check out, she realized the card Ruben gave was declined for the purchases. She began to panic in a frantic and called Ruben. She told him that her card was declined when she was trying to make a purchase at the store. Ruben said, "I know. I had your card cut off because you did not give me what I wanted or do what I asked you to do."

She told him, "OKAY," and hung up the phone. With embarrassment, she told the clerk that she had to leave the items because there was something wrong with her credit card. Sara was utterly ashamed of what had taken place.

"How could he do this to me?" She thought."

This is not what a husband is supposed to do. Just as she was walking off with the items left at the register and about to break down in the store, a sweet old lady came and tapped her on the shoulder. Sara turned around, and the lady said, "I have been here before, so please go back and pick up your items at the register. They have already been paid for you."

She broke down, and the sweet lady gave her the biggest hug and told her that no matter what was going on around her or what was happening to her, God had her back always. She wanted to get her information to thank the lady, but when Sara turned around, she was gone. The clerk informed Sara that this was taken care of and that an angel was in her midst. She got her items and had just enough to call a cab to pick her back up and take her home. When she arrived home, Ruben saw that she had a lot of bags and offered to help her; then hugged her and told her,

"I turned the credit card back on."

He acted as if nothing had happened. What in the world just happened? Sara was confused. Why was he being nice to her suddenly? He just made her look like a total fool when she went to the store, and now, he has restored the credit card and wants to give her a hug and help with the bags.

"Are you okay?" Sara asked Ruben in confusion.

"Yes, I am fine. Why do you ask?"

"Well, you didn't leave the keys in the car, and then when I went to the store, you had the card turned off so I wouldn't be able to use it."

"Well, I was just upset at the time."

"Really? Ruben, you cannot do that. Did you not ask me to quit my job so that you could take care of me? You made me look like a fool! I had to walk away from the counter and leave my groceries there because the card was declined. Not only that, but a sweet little lady also bought all the items that you are about to use, and all you have to say is I was upset at the time. Something is wrong with you!"

He went to give Sara a hug, and she pushed him off her because she didn't want him touching her. They both heard the doorbell.

"Are you expecting someone?"

"Yes, I was going to tell you that my sister was stopping by?"

"You had plenty of time for that."

Ruben went to answer the door, and Sara could hear his sister and him talk, and she brought the other little girls with her. Autumn listened to their voices and ran down, and the girls gave each other the biggest hug like they always do. Sara was still in her room and heard his sister say, I brought my two beautiful nieces with me. Sara heard this and came out of her room.

"If you cannot be nice, then just be quiet!"

Layla looked at Sara with shock on her face. "Yes, I heard you. I have addressed you plenty of times not to do this in front of my daughter. Do you not consider Autumn your beautiful niece? Autumn, go upstairs with your cousins for now."

"Okay, mom."

"I will ask the question again," Sara said. "Do you not consider Autumn your beautiful niece?"

The sister just stood in silence for a moment.

"Yes," she said in a low voice.

"Why do you keep doing this every time you are around?" Just as Sara was about to go off on the sister with her words, Ruben stopped her.

"I think if your sister cannot be nice, then she needs to stay away from the house until she knows how to act. How can anyone treat an innocent child like this?"

Sara and her siblings were raised in a household where they accepted everybody. It did not matter if the child was one of their siblings or not. That is not what their parents taught them. She could not understand why grown people would treat a little child who did not ask to be in this world and had no control over their circumstances be treated poorly and yet call themselves Christian, while having an ugly heart. It was Sara's belief if you have the love of Christ, then you would love and treat people right. Not these people! The next day when she went to the garage to go to the car, she discovered that the car was not out there.

"This is very strange," she said to herself.

"Where is the car?"

She asked Ruben and what came out of his mouth was very surprising. He told Sara that he had sold the car to his parents and that she needs to sign papers because they had already purchased it.

"You did what? Why would you do that?"

"You were getting another car anyway, so I told them they could buy it."

Sara didn't sign anything until she got a full understanding of what was going on. His mother came down to try and convince her that she needed to sign the papers. However, that conversation did not go over very well, and she still didn't sign the papers. She then proceeded to contact the bank and speak with the loan officer who started the paperwork on the vehicle. They informed her that Mrs. Mulberry now has ownership of the vehicle and explained to her what the papers meant. She informed Sara that she didn't want to get involved in any of the family drama. Mrs. Mulberry and her husband drove down to take the other vehicle back with them. Mrs. Mulberry told Sara that she and Ruben could get the car anytime that they needed to. Sara said to herself, "these are some trifling individuals. I mean you are driving a car that was supposedly supposed to be for your son's wife and daughters. You think that there is nothing wrong with that."

Ruben's dad acted as if he didn't want to drive the vehicle because he knew what they were doing was pure trash! Nevertheless, he went along with it anyway because Mrs. Mulberry had full control over the situation. He said he didn't want to drive the vehicle but did that stop him? NO! he drove it home anyway. Sara could not believe what was happening in front of her eyes. She has not seen something more pathetic than what her in laws were doing to her. By all means, Ruben was allowing this to happen. She spoke to Ruben and told him that he should rethink selling the car because they may need it when one of their cars break down. He didn't care! He was just going to do what mama said to do.

Sara eventually signed the papers since Mrs. Mulberry owned them at this point. She contacted a lawyer to see what she could do. He told her he could take the mom to court and fight her because Sara is the wife of Ruben. She thanked the lawyer for his advice but told him, it wasn't that serious and that she didn't want the car at this point. I mean, what could she do now? It didn't belong to her anymore. After she spoke to the lawyer and the loan officer, she signed the papers.

A few years went by, and Ruben's car broke down. He said,

"I should have kept the car."

Sara rolled her eyes and said,

"I told you not to sell it. What do I know? You never listen to me anyway, so I am not sure why you always want my input on things when you know you will just go and ask your mom. If mom says sell, then you sell, if mom says get a new one, then you will get it."

She then went out and got her a new car that Eduardo, Gustavo, and Mel helped her to get. Ruben couldn't take the fact that she had a new vehicle, even though he had sold her so-called car. He then threatened Sara that he wouldn't pay for anything of hers or the girls and that he would stop giving her money if she didn't allow him to co-sign.

"Why would you cosign Ruben? The bank is having a fantastic re-finance option. You don't have a car to refinance since yours is paid off."

She later learned that Mrs. Mulberry called her son and put the idea in his head. This was just another way that woman would try to control Sara through Ruben. How can someone be so wicked? Sara thought this woman needed to go and fix her own marriage and find out why her husband is always drinking and staying on his phone as if he couldn't put it down for one second. I know he isn't talking to his homies like that. She rolled her eyes and told Ruben no. He got mad at Sara and did what he did best, throw a temper tantrum to try and control her.

Mrs. Mulberry and Ruben would stop at nothing to try and get Sara to do what they wanted her to do.

The family set the tone at the beginning of how they treated Sara and Autumn. They didn't like her from day one. Mrs. Mulberry was good about pretending she loved her and cared for her so much when she was around other people. When she gets Sara by herself, she begins to talk to her like she is dumb and says stuff that she shouldn't. She doesn't want to deal with anyone else's children unless they are blood-related. Sara often wondered if this was how she treated her in laws. Even if it was, she should know better than to come into someone's home and act the way she does and say what she does. She is a disrespectful woman, and all Sara wanted was respect! Sara wanted the same treatment that she had shown to others to be shown to her.

She wasn't rude to them and always welcomed them into her home. She wouldn't go to their homes and be disrespectful to them. It was tough for her to understand why they would do that at her home. Then, she realized they did this because Ruben would allow them to be disrespectful.   Then have the nerve to go and say "Amen" and take communion with all that filth and hate in their hearts. They may be fooling other people, but they were not fooling Sara. She could see right through them. She could feel their evil spirits. Every time she knew that they were coming, she would always have dreams right before they would show up of either snakes or spiders. She often anointed her home with holy oil before they got there, so maybe that is why they never could get too comfortable and couldn't stay too long.

She couldn't change a person; only God could. Sara stayed away from the family until they learned how to be respectful. She did not answer any phone calls or text messages. If there were any family gatherings, she made sure to stay away. This went on for a few years. She knew the only person she could lean on was Jesus. She prayed and prayed. Things seemed to be looking up, or so she thought. Maybe they were getting somewhere at one point, then here comes the bomb.

It was like the scenarios kept repeating themselves. Why did she keep putting herself in these situations? She knew early on that Ruben was not for her, but she disregarded all the warning signs. She was miserable and felt isolated from her family and friends. When she wanted her family to come and visit, Ruben would always make it seem as if it was a problem and give her rules for what they could or couldn't do and use and not use. However, it seemed the limits were off when it came to his family. It seemed that when they came to visit, they could have whatever they wanted and eat at expensive restaurants when they wanted. They also got to use whatever they liked. Why was her family treated differently? His family, he thought, deserved the finer things. They also got away with many things that were not acceptable to Sara. Ruben didn't care at all.

However, he tried to limit Sara's family to a very strict budget. Her family hardly ever came around because of how heartless Ruben would act toward them. One day her parents were watching tv at the house, and Ruben began to vacuum right in the middle of their show. He showed disrespect when it came to Sara's parents.

Sara never really told anyone what was going on. Yes, they would call, but she never told them what was going on. However, she knew that some of them had a feeling about what was happening and were waiting for her to speak up. They had tried to warn Sara early on, but she thought she knew best. The stress of Ruben, Mrs. Mulberry, and Layla began to take a toll on Sara's health. She was allowing the stress of Ruben and his family to get to her. Her hair began to fall out, and parts of her body began to swell up unexpectedly. Her joints began to hurt, and she began to get migraine headaches and panic attacks. Things were going from bad to worse.

Mrs. Mulberry came over again. It seemed she would always come when Layla or their brother came. Sara went to lie down and decided to give Ruben and his family space. Again, she overheard the brother tell Ruben she's not trying to say her children are yours, is she? She looks nothing like you! Wow! Sara thought to herself. What is he trying to say? Just then, she walked out of her room, and they quickly became quiet. Sara spoke to everyone and decided not to entertain what was said. She was learning to pick and choose her battles.

Mrs. Mulberry talked to Sara and wanted to know when she would get her college degree. "My son knows he needs to marry someone educated and has a very good paying job because you will not have my son go bankrupt!" She told Sara.

"Are you serious right now? If your son goes bankrupt, it will be because of him. Y'all are out of your mind! Why do you even call yourself Christian? I mean, you sit there and quote scriptures, but on the inside, your heart is very ugly. You should be ashamed of yourself."

Sara finally spoke up to Mrs. Mulberry.

"Please understand this is not disrespect because I was taught better than that. Why are you comfortable with putting me down? Do you have no conviction? Let me guess; you don't. You can't have any and talk and treat me any way and think that's okay. Time after time, I have asked you all to be respectful when coming to visit, and you continue to treat me and my daughter with such disrespect. Please do not come back until all of you can be respectful. Y'all are very ridiculous with an ugly heart. You think God is pleased with that? You talk about me and put me down. Your lives must be miserable at this point. I am convinced."

She could tell they were boiling over with anger, and she didn't care. Ruben told Sara not to talk to his family like that. Never did he stick up for Sara. Then again, Ruben never stood up for Sara. She was always left to defend herself. He cared if she was disrespectful to his family but never cared if they were rude to her. If she tried to tell him, he would justify their behavior and say, they didn't mean it that way, or that's just how they are. She got tired of it. This is what he would say repeatedly.

Sara started to feel weak. She made an appointment with the doctor to get a checkup because she knew her health was in jeopardy. They examined her and took blood samples. As Sara waited patiently for the results, she began to pray and call upon those who she knew were prayer warriors. They began to pray with her and for her. The doctor came into the room and told Sara that they should have the results in a few days. One of the things Sara began to do was journal. She knew if she journaled, she could get her anger out on paper. She took out her journal from her desk drawer and began to write.

May 2014, 11:30 pm, A word to the wise: Never overlook a person's pattern, behavior, or how they make you feel. If you are getting a bad vibe, it is not for any reason. You are getting that because there is danger up ahead and God is trying to warn you before you get too invested into a situation. Ask me how I know? I was one who ignored the signs too. There were signs coming from all different directions and people.

Chapter 11

The day Sara was getting married, she had an accident. Even though she had an accident, she still ignored this as her sign not to marry the man she thought she wanted. A person will show you one side when you are dating, and then when you marry them, it will be a whole different person, or so you think. The person has been who they always were, and they did not manifest themselves fully until they have trapped you. I do not know if this has happened to anyone else, and maybe you married someone who is the same. Signing off! She always ended her writing with signing off or being blessed. She put her pin down, closed her journal, and put it back in the nightstand drawer. To herself, she wondered where did this person come from? You will pay for being disobedient, she said to herself. She then remembered Deuteronomy 28 and how it talks about curses for being disobedient.

However, she did not see this side of him until after she married him. She felt this was her punishment for disobeying the warning signs. She was not happy, and even though she was married, she felt very lonely. This is not what she signed up for. She thought she was getting the man of her dreams, but this was turning out to be a nightmare! The abuse (not physically) was not only coming from her husband but also from his family!

There were plenty of times she had to pause and let them know how she felt. They were talking about her and treating her and her daughter poorly, and Ruben allowed the behavior. A plethora of times she informed her husband with what was being said or done to her and Autumn and he would just justify his family's behavior or get irate with her if she said one word about his family. The Bible says in *Ephesians 5:31 For this reason a man shall leave his father and mother and be joined to his wife, and the two shall become one flesh (NKJV).*

Sara assumed that he knew this information since he was raised in a Christian home. He was still cleaving on to his mother. He could not even set healthy boundaries with his family because he assumed he would be disrespectful towards them if he did this. She went through this for years with the disrespect of her husband and his mom.

"Why do I put up with this?" She thought to herself. She knew this was not what she wanted and wanted to get out of the marriage, but she did not think she had any options because she didn't believe in divorce and thought God would be highly upset with her if she left him for this.

Sara stayed and took the mess! She confided in her friend circle, and they wanted her to get out of the situation and agreed to let Autumn and Joy come and stay with them for a while because they didn't want either of the girls around the chaos. Honestly, she told herself there was no way out, and if it was, how would she make it?

The one thing that kept her from moving on was her finances. At the time, she was at a job that did not pay very well, and then Ruben asked her to quit and that he would take care of her and the girls. When she inquired about government assistance, they told Sara that she did not qualify for it. She was starting to get bored not having anything to do, and she felt like she was wasting time and life was passing her by. Every day was not bad. There were some good days she and Ruben had. However, she just did not see a way out of the mess that she got herself into. She began to start looking at colleges/universities to help occupy her time.

As she was looking, she received a phone call from Dr. Goddard. He informed Sara that she had an autoimmune disease that was causing her swelling, and she also had anemia and a low iron deficiency, which all of that together caused her to be very lethargic at times. They gave her recommendations on what she could do to help improve her health and wanted her to go and get treatments for low iron. She hung up the phone with the doctor and called Eduardo, Gustavo, Allison, and Mel to inform them of the news.

They informed Sara that they would continue to pray for complete healing over her body. Before Sara got off the phone, they began to pray for Sara, Autumn, and Joy. Before the call ended, they all said they loved each other as they always do. Sara began to cry because she missed her family and friends and felt like she was in a place of isolation.

She wiped the tears from her eyes and encouraged herself. "You got this, girl! God will not give you more than you can bear! I am healed, delivered, and set free in Jesus' name!"

She logged back onto her laptop and began to continue her research with colleges/universities that she was interested in. She thought about enrolling in the university that she was suspended from. After all, she liked to prove people wrong. They didn't think Sara was college material or that she was smart enough to continue her education and suggested that she enlist in the military. Others would tell her that she wasn't smart enough or that she was in her thirties and still trying to get a degree. The words of the naysayers still rang loud in her ear. After she sat for a while and thought about it, she decided to enroll back into the university she was attending before getting married. She contacted the university to find out what she needed to do. She would need to write an appeal, and this appeal would need to grab the hearts of the committee and move them. Sara wasted no time. She began to write because school would be starting soon.

Time had flown by, and Sara was finally finished with her letter. She doubled checked it for errors and made sure that it sounded exceptional. She hit the submit button and hoped and prayed for the best. Once that was complete, she contacted Mel because she was going to pick up Autumn and Joy. They were going to drive home and visit her parents. Once she arrived, her parents were overjoyed to see she and the girls because they had not seen them in a while. They hugged, laughed, and talked, but Sara did not let them know everything that was happening because she did not want them to worry. It was getting late, and they all were getting hungry. They drove to Benny Bill's restaurant to eat. They were waiting for the hostesses to seat them at a table. Sara knew exactly what she was going to order, and the girls always got the same thing. Chicken strips and French fries, sweet tea, and Dr. Pepper for Joy.

As they were waiting, they ate rolls and talked about new and old things; just as they were getting into their conversation, the food finally came out. The aroma was everything and brought Sara back to her childhood. As they sat down and ate, Sara kept noticing an older lady staring at their table. She wondered why the woman kept staring at her, but she tried to ignore it and kept talking and eating. She looked up again, but the woman approached their table this time. She said, "I kept noticing you over here, and your beautiful daughters, and I want to know if I can prophesy to you."

Sara looked at her mom, and her mom said Yes.

She told her that the thing she was worried about was already worked out. Sara was in shock because this lady did not know her, and she did not know this woman. After she spoke about what God had given her, the lady walked off. Sara knew exactly what she was worried about, so she knew it was God. Once they were done eating, they got in the car and headed back home. Sara was sitting on the couch and just happened to check her email. What she found next made her leap up for joy. It was the email from the committee of the university she applied for.

The email read: Congratulations! On your admission to our school.

She jumped up, ran, and told her dad because her mom went to the store. Her dad was just as excited as she was. He hugged her and told her he was happy for her. When her mom finally showed she was so excited and when she got excited, her voice got loud and high pitched. She told Sara that she was proud of her. That is what Sara was worried about whether she would get into the university.

God came through like he did the last time for her, and she had a lot to be thankful for. It was almost nightfall, and Sara, Autumn, and Joy had to get back on the road and go home. For a moment, Sara had joy return to her. She and the girls arrived only to find Ruben not there. Sara walked in with a sigh of relief that he wasn't there. She didn't have to listen to him whine or nag her about what was messed up or what wasn't done. Just a little bit of peace made all the difference for her. Autumn and Joy washed up and then went to bed for the night. The girls told their mom they loved her, prayed for her, and were happy. Tears filled Sara's eyes, but she held them back because she did not want Autumn or Joy to see her cry. Just as she was getting relaxed in walks Ruben. Sara saw him and turned away, and rolled her eyes.

"You can't speak," he asked.

She told him, "Well, you're the one coming into the door, so maybe you should speak."

Sara did not want to argue, so she apologized and said,

"Yes, I should have spoken to you; please forgive me."

She did not want anything or anyone to disrupt the joy that she had. Ruben began to make small talk with her, and Sara was over it. She was at the point where she started not to like him. This was because of all the verbal and emotional abuse he and his mom were causing her. He went into their bedroom to get ready for bed, and this made Sara happy because she could finally be to herself without him breathing down her neck. It was now 2:00 am, and Sara knew she needed to go to bed, but she was enjoying the downtime and wanted to catch up on her shows. She kneeled beside the couch to pray before going to bed. She sometimes felt that God was not listening to her. There were plenty of times she wanted to give up and throw in the towel and say,

"Whatever happens, happens! Because God is not listening anyway. This is a trick of the enemy! He will lead you to believe that God is not there and that he has abandoned you, so that you will give up on God. The enemy hopes that you do not reach your destined place and hopes that you will get off focus or off track because he thinks he has you."

She had mental breakdowns and almost grew to the point of rage against her husband and his family. It had gotten to the point where she did not care anymore. The attacks kept coming! She did not care what happened to him or his family members because all Ruben wanted to do was control her because he was the breadwinner of the home.

Sara wanted them to suffer how they made her suffer. His mother came to visit one day, and she opened her mouth to speak words that were vile towards she and her daughter. She couldn't take it anymore and took the keys, but just as she was about to get in the car, Ruben and his mother came to the garage to stop her from leaving. She held onto Joy to not let her go while Sara was trying to take her away, and Ruben tried to take the keys from Sara, but they went under her car, and she grabbed them quickly and pulled on his shirt to move him out the way. All this was happening while his mother looked on standing from the garage door. Sara looked at her and said,

"You see what your son is doing, and all your doing is standing there?" Mulberry replied,

"I don't want to get involved," but she had already involved herself when she opened her mouth to speak evil toward Sara.

Words were exchanged, and Sara got in Mrs. Mulberry's face and pointed her finger, and told her this is you and your sons doing, and you are a liar! She told her how her son needed to get off her breast milk. At that point, Mrs. Mulberry told Ruben that he could do whatever he wanted. Ruben told Sara with a loud voice that she could file for divorce.

She said, "You file since you're the one wanting a divorce."

He tried to be big and bad, and yet he didn't even want to file the divorce. Sara took Autumn and

Joy and got in her car, and drove to Eduardo and Gustavo house. She and the girls arrived at Eduardo and Gustavo's home. They ran to her and hugged her very tightly. They had their room ready for them and told Sara to stay. They wanted Sara and the girls to rest. Before getting in bed, Sara knelt down and began praying.

The two brothers were furious about what happened and hated most of all that Autumn and Joy were there. Sara had to repent for the thoughts she had towards them and the words that were spoken. She knew that was not God reflected in her, and that was not the way to be. Sara remembered what her mom Sybil told her years ago to pray and ask God to change her. At the time, Sara was like, why would I do that? They are the ones that need to change. They are the ones coming for me and my children. She did not understand why her mom would tell her that.

Nevertheless, she began to pray, "Lord, change me for the better."

She would pray this prayer because if they saw the change in her, they would eventually want to change or begin to change as she hoped. She kept allowing them to provoke her and take her to a place where she did not want to go. If she lives for the Lord, she's supposed to reflect God, and she knew she was not always reflecting Him.

Sara said, "God are you hearing me? Why aren't they changing? Or why doesn't it feel like I am changing?"

She wanted things to speed along. However, God's timing is not our timing. He shows up on his time, which is always on time! Sara kept praying, "God, if you give me the green light, then I will leave."

One day, she was browsing the internet and went onto periscope and came across this pastor, and she could not turn away from the screen nor turn it off because she was speaking facts! As she was saying it, it was ministering to her soul. She began to follow her. One day, she called Sara's name on the live broadcast and told her that she had been through the fire but was getting ready to come out. Hallelujah! To God be all the glory. She did not know this woman of God, nor did she know Sara. God knew! When she said this, she immediately knew what she was talking about. All the time, God was listening to her, but she had to suffer because of her disobedience she felt. Sara began to cry and thanked God for hearing her. She pulled out her journal and began to write.

August 25, 2019, Important to note:

When God tells you to do something, then do it! If he gives you signs and warnings, then obey him. He knows what trouble lies ahead that you do not know. It is important to take heed to what God is saying.

Despite all she had gone through, she was determined to finish her education. She battled with the voices in her head telling her that she wasn't good enough or smart enough, or that she was too old.

However, she fought through the noise and believed in God for the best in her life. When you are determined to do something, you will do it despite your circumstances, she told herself. It does not matter what others say because no demon in hell can block what God has called you to do. Oh! they will try, but it will not work. The Bible tells us *Isaiah 54:17 (KJV) No Weapon formed against you shall prosper, and every tongue which rises against you in judgement shall be condemned.*

Chapter 12

arlier, Sara was praying for God to change her. Soon enough, she began to feel the change on the inside of her. She could not quite put her finger on it, but she knew God was up to something amazing in her life. One night, she was sitting on the couch, and Ruben's father wanted to talk to her about a licensing question because Sara used to work for a mortgage company. However, she did not feel led to speak with him, and Ruben began to explode on her. Sara did not know what was going on or what this feeling was that came over her. She then thought, "Is this me, or is this you, Lord?"

It was that night she clearly heard to separate herself from Ruben and his family. She did not understand at the time. She began to block his family members because they were toxic toward her. She knew she had to get away from the place that she was in that had caused her so much pain and heartache, and loneliness, but she did not know how or when she was to leave. During all of this, her health began to get worse. Her feet, ankles, and hands would swell up all the time, and she had panic attacks and asthma attacks that would appear out of nowhere, although she has not had those for years. Her hair started to fall out to the point where she ended up with bald spots because she was stressing badly. They did not know the damage they were causing her. Sara's husband did not know to what extent this was causing her. All she knew that night, she had to do something to get her peace back, so she blocked them.

She can remember reaching out to the woman of God she found on social media because she did not know what to do. She shared with Sara some things that God told her. It was life changing. She did not know what Sara was going through, but God revealed it to her. The green light Sara had asked God for had finally come. It was scary for her at first because she had not been alone for many years. She was obedient to what God told her and began to search for a home for herself and her daughters. She desperately looked and applied for an apartment, although she wanted a house. She did not care because desperation had set in. At that moment, all she could think about was getting out of a bad situation. She filled out the apartment application only to get declined. She was very appalled.

"God, Really?" She thought to herself. "I can't even get an apartment. Like, what is up with that?" The apartment was small, but she told herself, "It will do for now."

Her baby girl knew she was frustrated and disappointed that she did not get it. Joy looked at her mom and told her,

"It is okay, mom; you will find something bigger and better!"

Out of the mouths of babies, God speaks! Let's look for places over the weekend her daughter said. She went to bed, trying not to worry about it, but she still did not understand why she got turned down. The next morning, she got up and began her search on the internet while Ruben was away at his parent's house for the weekend. She found a place that looked very nice and was in a nice, well-kept neighborhood. She told herself this must be the house! Sara dreamed of what the house would look like and how many bedrooms. All she knew she was looking for a home that had a blue accent wall because that is what was shown to her.

Finally, she reached out to the property manager and went and looked at the home. It was much bigger and better, as her daughter told her. She looked in rooms and noticed that there was a blue accent wall. Ah! This is it! This is what I saw in my dream. Then she began to get scared because what if they rejected me for this place? Or what if I don't meet the income requirements? Every scenario she could think of went through her head. She knew if God said it, then it was settled. When he speaks, it changes and moves things! If he tells you to go, then he will provide for you. She had her faith to hold onto and needed to be vital for Autumn and Joy, but Autumn and Joy were being strong for her too. She knew that God would never get her out of something and leave her hanging or struggling. He is the God that always provides. It may not come how you expect it because we are always looking for it to reach a certain way, but sometimes God will send it a different way.

Allison told Sara to go ahead and put the application in for the house because she knew Sara was hesitant. She gave Sara the funds for the application fee and told her to fill out the application now! Not thinking anything negative about it, she put in the application and said, "Okay, Lord, you told me to separate myself, so you must open this door."

Within a few hours, she was approved for her very own place. It was not an apartment but a house. Sara knew at that moment that God wanted to give her the best. Not that apartments were wrong, but Sara knew what she needed to fit her needs. She was in awe of how God moved so quickly and how things just worked themselves out. Sara was dumbfounded because how was she approved for this home and rejected for the apartment she looked at?

When God is in it, He is going to give you, His best! She wanted to be close to the neighborhood the family home was in because she wanted the girls to be in the same school district. God honored all of that and blessed her with a new job making more money! This was prophecy being fulfilled all because Sara obeyed God. When you are obedient to what God tells you to do, in Deuteronomy 28 KJV, as mentioned earlier, Jesus will command the blessing upon your life, and your baskets will be packed and overflowing.

Sara could not begin to tell anyone how much joy she had and how being obedient increased her faith. She had mustard seed faith, but when she obeyed, it elevated her faith from mustard seed faith to faith that moves mountains. God continues to blow her mind all because she stepped out and obeyed. The next hurdle would be to get out of the lake house. She knew Ruben would not want her to move and would do everything he could to block her from leaving. She needed him to be away from home so that she could get her things.

How would she tell him that she is separating herself from him? How would he react? She never knew if she would get pleasant Ruben or unpleasant Ruben. While Ruben went to visit his parents, she began to gather up some of her things and take them to her new house. Eduardo, Allison, Mel, and Gustavo took time out of their day to come and help her move as much stuff as they could before he got back. Once she got most of her things moved, she went back to the lake house to gather more, only to find Ruben at home.

"Hi, how was your trip?" she asked.

"It was fine. You want to tell me what you're doing right now?"

"What do you mean?"

"Your things are gone. Are you moving out?"

"Well, yes, that is what I wanted to talk to you about."

Why are you moving out?"

"I think you know, Ruben. I mean, you continue to disrespect me, and you allow your family to treat me like garbage too. I must always defend myself when it comes to them because of some lie you have told. Plus, you like to control me, and I do not have time for it. It is very tiring to walk on eggshells because I don't know what will set you off."

Sara began to count down, starting with 5, 4, 3, 2, 1, and he's off! Sure enough, Ruben began to yell and be angry at Sara. Each time he wouldn't get his way; this is what he did. He would be hateful to her and then treat her as if nothing ever happened and began to shower her with gifts. He looked at her and told her he didn't want her to leave. She told Ruben this was something that she had to do. I know how I want to be treated, and you're not treating me how I want. Am I able to continue to spend time with the girls? Yes, if that is what they want. I will have movers come to get the rest of my things tomorrow. He began to beg Sara not to leave him, but she ignored him and kept walking out the door.

Sara knew that things between her and Ruben were not getting better and that he was toxic. She spent time getting her place together, and she and Autumn would go shopping and pick out things for her room. Sara unlocked her phone and blocked those people that were not meant for her good. She sometimes would not answer family members because she was going through a lot. She wanted to drown out all the noise and lean and listen for the voice of God. Once she did that, her health began to improve. She knew it was from being in a toxic environment. Sara knew that she had to get away. She had peace of mind, and Joy and Autumn were resting better than they had ever rested because being in that environment affected them too. Sara took out her journal just before she began a new task. She always made time to journal.

October 2019 12:15 a.m. When you know how you want to be treated, you will make your demands. If they cannot treat you how you want and deserve to be treated, then it may be time for you to re-evaluate that situation and move on!

Chapter 13

Ruben would call Sara just about every day to try and convince her to come back home. He told her how much he missed her and the girls and that he was sorry for everything and wanted to work on things. However, Sara was not moved by his words. She needed to see action, and so far, he hadn't shown her any movement toward a better relationship. He wanted to go to counseling, but Sara did not want to go because they had gone before, which did not work out well. She didn't want to waste time and money only for the relationship to end back where it was or worse off. She told him that was not an option for her. This was not an easy process for Sara. She had to continue to pray and ask God to change her because he was continuously working on her. She had to get to a place and decide if she would continue to be bitter or want to become a better version of herself.

Did she want to hold on to the past about what he and his family had said or done? No, she wanted to let all of it go because holding on to it was not acceptable. She had to learn to forgive and truly forgive and let go of the past hurts and pains. She had to get to a place where they could talk about her without being affected or bothered by what they said. This wasn't easy, but she knew she could do it.

"God is still working on me," she said. She knew her peace was more important than listening to the outside voices.

When you have peace, you will do what you must to protect it. Sara had to repent for what she said and did in the relationship. She knew that you cannot blame everything on the other person. She had to examine herself, too, forgive herself for allowing certain things to happen, and forgive herself for her poor choice of words and thoughts that she knew were not good.

II Corinthians 13:5 (KJV), *Examine yourselves, whether ye be in the faith; prove your own selves. Know ye not your own selves, how that Jesus Christ is in you except ye be reprobates?*

It is very hard to want to deal with someone that has oppressed you. She wanted to get revenge on them. There are some things that she could have gotten them back on but what good would that have done? She knew the battle belonged to God and he will repay.

Romans 12:19 (KJV) says *Dearly beloved, avenge not yourselves, but rather give place unto wrath: for it, is written Vengeance is mine; I will repay, saith the Lord.*

Every time she wanted to take things into her own hands, she would open her Bible, and God would speak a word to her. Sara had to back off. She had to trust that Jesus had it under control and that silence is sometimes best. She could have gone back and forth with them and continued to have rage like she used to do, but she knew that her peace was worth far more than that. She has learned to shut her mouth and let God fight her battles. That does not mean she is a pushover or will let them run over her and try to control her. She had to set boundaries! Sara had to learn to be alright even if they never told her they were sorry. She struggled with this a lot. She asked herself,

"How can someone mistreat you and then want to be in your presence and smooth it over with food and gifts?"

This was very strange to her. Growing up, she and her family apologized for their words and actions. However, Sara had to learn to forgive despite of what they said or did. She imagined what her in-laws would be like, and it was nothing how she pictured it. She dreamed they would be saved, sanctified, and filled with the Holy Ghost. That they would be people of their word, love, speak life, pray for and pray over her, the children, and her husband, that they would have discernment and be able to tell them things and see things that she or her husband couldn't see. She wanted them to love her for who she was and love the girls despite them not being the biological children and treat them as if they were their very own grandchildren. She wanted she and her mother-in-law and sister- in-law to be able to hang out and get along as if they were the best of friends. If they had a disagreement, she wanted to be able to sit down and talk about the issues in love without anyone getting hurt and wanted to be able to shop and go to church with each other. These are the things Sara had hoped for.

Instead, she got the opposite. She couldn't help but think what her life would have been like if she had just waited on God to send her helpmate and taken heed to all the warning signs that were sent to her. Sometimes she'd often daydream of the real man God had for her and the real in-laws that would be in her and Autumn and Joy's lives and how they would love them. For now, she had to get through what she was dealing with. She had to allow God to continue to do the work in her and through her and forgive herself and forgive them. She knew this wouldn't be an easy task for her. She was willing to go through the process and heal. Ruben kept texting her and calling her to come over. He never really cooked for her, but he called and told her that he would cook dinner because he just wanted to talk to her. Sara knowing his tactics, simply ignored him. She knew they had nothing to really talk about. She had decisions to make about getting a divorce from him. She turned Ruben down for dinner. She was not ready to face him or have him affect her peace. Sara thought, "How can someone treat an innocent child so poorly? Secondly, why did Ruben's mom think she could come into our home and do whatever she wanted to do and say whatever she wanted to say?"

Now that Sara was in her own place, she had time to think about things and had peace. According to *II Corinthians 6:17 (KJV) Wherefore come out from among them and be ye separate.*

Sara felt like she couldn't breathe while living at the lake house and being in an atrocious situation. It was a feeling she had not felt in a very long time, and she did not have to be bothered by text messages or phone calls. She sat in her chair and began to reminisce on things and how she felt at peace. She felt God had lifted the heaviness from her. She didn't want to allow Ruben or any of his family members to take her peace again because her peace was worth fighting for! Her time away helped her to realize that she could love and pray for people from a distance. Yes, they mistreated her, but she was at a place where she could be cordial and fix you a plate to go but would not allow you in her home. That doesn't mean she did not love them or would not be there for them if they needed her to be. She continues to pray for him and his family. She thought, I don't have to be friends with them, nor do I have to be enemies either.

Sitting down and thinking about these things, she began to write in her journal.

November 19, 2019, Let's talk about boundaries. According to Merriam-Webster dictionary, boundaries-are something that indicates or fixes a limit or extent. Boundaries are something I have always had but had difficulty getting across to family members, in-laws, friends, and associates. I thought if I told them no or told them how I felt or that they could not do this or that, it meant I was being mean. For this, people will take advantage of my kindness and think that they could just run over me, and I would be accepting of this. I know I allowed this to go on for too long. It began to irritate me after a while that people thought they could come into my home or space and think they had a right to just enter every room without permission or talk about my family while visiting me. I allowed this type of behavior from them because I simply wanted to avoid an argument. I wanted to keep the peace and enjoyed the peace to be held between my family and Ruben's family. There were times I would boil over with anger because of things that were said or done. I felt like I was in a fight all by myself. I did not have anyone to defend me when Karen wanted to start chaos! Knowing how this woman treated my daughter and me it would make anyone want to pull their hair out and call it quits. However, Ruben did not understand or think his mother could do such horrendous acts. Sometimes I'd tell him, and he would justify it as, "oh, that's just how she is."

Or she's not mean like that. Sara never understood why her husband could not stick up for her and then got mad when she defended herself and defended Autumn. This caused significant havoc in their home, and he and Sara were always arguing. There must be healthy boundaries that you and your spouse must set when it comes to each other's family. Family members should not be able to come into your home or vice versa and say or do what they want to do. If you give them permission that is different.

This type of behavior can cause damage to your marriage and relationships. Both spouses need to sit down and talk about what healthy boundaries you would like to see and want when it comes to each other's family. Remember, you both will need to ensure that both of you are doing your part so that when friends or family come over, they do not disrespect you or your spouse. I had to learn the hard way. It is still an adjustment, and I am still a work in progress but with God, I know it will get better for me, even if that means being without Ruben. His mother and sister Layla still say stuff on the sly and do things in subtle ways. They still take little digs at me. They know exactly what they are doing and choose to do it anyway. In a way, it can be exhausting demanding respect from people who never respected you to begin with.

When you are in someone's home, then you should respect the person and their home, just as you would want them to respect you and your home. Most of the times I sit quietly and take mental notes. Ruben still has issues defending her most of the time and still makes me out to look like the person he painted in the beginning to his family. Many would say this is narcissistic behavior and I agree. No one should have to put up with a toxic husband or toxic in-laws that do not mean you any good. Signing Off for the night!

Sara had been putting up with this kind of behavior for many years. They never really got to know her and didn't want to get to know her. They wanted still to see her in the eyes of their son. They could only see the person that Ruben made her out to be. How could someone not get to know a person for themselves? Why would they go by someone else's perception of them? This baffled Sara. She endured mistreatment from his mother, father, sister, and brother. Now, the father -n-law did not do that much, but he would make little rude comments about Sara.

However, they cater to Ruben's brother's wife, Rachel, a lot. The difference in their relationship is that Joseph didn't speak negative things to his family about her. This made a world of difference in how they treated Rachel and Sara. Ruben's mother swears she doesn't treat either of her daughter-in-laws any differently. How can she not see that she does mistreat Sara? She sits down with Ruben's wife and talk to her and tells her the latest gossip or tries to find out information or is there for her when she needs it. She tries to take the load off her.

Sara, on the other hand, is left out and her feelings do not matter. No one ever asked Sara if she is doing well or if she needs anything. They never seem to see the frustration or pain on her face. They do not care if she is stressed out. When she tried to tell Ruben, he would just get upset with her and fuss at her. When Rachel says, "I am stressed", everyone seems to run to her and help lift the load off her whether its, taking her children to give her some time to herself or helping around the house. Whatever she needs they seem to make it easy for her, while Sara is left on her own. Always fighting and defending herself, always having to be strong, tough, and trying to make her voice be heard. She always tried to not let her emotions get the best of her. All they saw was a strong independent woman who could handle herself.

Sometimes, Sara needed them to ask what can we help you with? Or I can see that you're stressed, what do you need? It wasn't so much that it was her in-laws, but she needed Ruben to inform them that she was stressed or she was tired to help ease the load like Joseph would do with Rachel. Instead, he always took his family's side, and Sara is left there looking dumb because he acts like he knows nothing and doesn't do anything.

He went off on Sara one day because of the information he received from his brother. Sara had to try to understand what it was about. She asked him, and he told her that Rachel was stressed because they were trying to get things together for their party. Instead of Ruben just telling her that Rachel is stressed, he went off on Sara. He made it seem like she was asking him too many questions or that he couldn't tell her what was happening. She had to keep probing to get the answers that she needed. This is the type of behavior she had to deal with.

Sara always felt like she was left to fight and defend herself with no help. No one comes to her rescue, but they will come up against her, talk about her, and speak things that are not true, while her husband sits down alongside them and joins in the conversation instead of defending his wife. No man or woman should have to deal with this behavior. This is not what married couples are supposed to do or how they should act. How can you say, "You love me to your wife or husband and then turn around and allow the mistreatment to continue?" Any mistreatment by the husband, wife, or by in-laws is wrong!

Ephesians 4:25 says, Husbands, love your wives, even as Christ also loved the church, and gave himself for it.

How can we say we have the love of God, but we treat each other with so much disrespect and have ill will towards each other? This is not how a marriage is supposed to be. There must be harmony, and unity, and there must be RESPECT! You cannot say you love God and then go and mistreat your spouse. This does not only apply to marriages, but it applies to all your relationships. Healthy boundaries will need to be established between both parties. How can a marriage or relationship survive if there are no boundaries, love, trust, or respect? How can it survive if the husband or wife is constantly allowing family members to disrespect their spouse? A person can only take so much until they have reached their boiling point or until one of you decides to walk away. Sara did not want to allow Ruben to continue to mishandle her. Therefore, she moved on because of the turmoil, stress, worry, and fear. She knew she had to get out of there not only for her but for Joy and Autumn too. This is not the type of environment she wanted her baby girls to grow up in. She knew it wouldn't be easy, but she knew it would be worth it.

Chapter 14

It was getting closer to thanksgiving, and she had so many things to do. She thought about having her parents and friends over at her new place. It would be the first holiday that would be spent in her home. Autumn and Joy were away with Sara's grandparents, and they would come home for thanksgiving. By this time, Autumn is now thirteen, and Joy is 11. Both girls enjoy being around their grandparents with whom she calls G-ma and G- pop. They knew that they have other grandparents, Autumn was not able to communicate with her biological dad's grandparents because they are missing in action. She has Ruben's grandparents, but she does not really see them as grandparents because of how they treated her mother and her.

Out of respect from what her mother taught her, she respects and loves them, but she is not very close to them. The most important people in her life are her mom, her G-ma, and G-pop. She is very close to them. Those are the only grandparents that she considers true and real grandparents. She was their baby and still is their baby girl. Whatever Autumn and Joy needs they make sure that they are well and able to provide for them. She is always talking to them about certain things and asking them questions. She is constantly learning from them because she knows that they are full of wisdom and knowledge. If she has learned anything from her mom over the years, she has learned to listen to wisdom and always, always pray!

Autumn and Joy would love to have a close knit relationship with Ruben's parents, but they have made it hard for her to trust them by their behavior and the words they speak. When his parents or siblings think that she is not listening, she is. She is listening and looking at everything that they do. She has lost all trust in Ruben and tells her mom to get out of the situation as fast as possible. She and Joy hated seeing her mom treated and talked about so poorly. She knew that what they were saying was not the mother that was raising them into beautiful, bright, intelligent young women.

Whenever she sees Ruben, she is standoffish, and when she speaks to him, she speaks at a low volume because she doesn't like him. Surely Ruben could not be this ignorant not to notice that Autumn's behavior has changed towards him. Maybe it wasn't that he was ignorant of it; maybe it is that he sees the change in her and doesn't want to admit it. He would try to do silly things and say silly things that would normally make a child smile, but Autumn was not moved nor impressed.

She would just usually give him a half smile or a low wave or say hello in her monotone voice, usually to where he could barely hear her. This was because she didn't really care for him. One day while helping her mother in the kitchen with food, she wanted to talk to her mom about him. She told Sara that it is hard for her to try and like him or act as if she does anyway. She told her,

"Mom, I try really hard, but this is very hard for me."

Sara knew where her daughter was coming from. Autumn knew he was the only dad that she ever had because her biological father was in and out, and then he went missing. She tried to like him, but this was an area she was struggling with. She and her mom would pray like they always do because they were each other's strength. Sometimes, Autumn would talk to her mom, and she spoke with so much wisdom that Sara was in awe of how well her daughter spoke. Other times, she knew that God was speaking through her daughter to her. This is what it was for Autumn when her mom would talk to her. Sara wanted to give her daughters the same strong Godly foundation that her parents gave her. Lean on the rock, which is Christ Jesus and she wanted her daughters to do the same.

It was two days before Thanksgiving, and Sara had a lot to do. She did not do this on her own because she had help from her best friends Eduardo and Gustavo. They could always help her because they ran a successful business, and Pinky's was named the most favorite and authentic coffee shop! Sara loved to see her friends getting blessed, and they always celebrated with each other. She had sent the brothers on errands for her while she continued to decorate and get things for the holiday. While she was decorating her home, Ruben called her. She let it ring and go to voicemail. He called her right back, and she decided to answer the phone.

"Hi, Ruben."

"Well, hello, Sara, how are you?"

"I am doing well. What is going on?"

"I wanted to see if you had any plans for thanksgiving and if not, then would you and Autumn join me for dinner?"

"Thank you for the invite. However, we have plans for thanksgiving dinner."

Ruben kept trying to persuade her to come over, but Sara would not bulge.

"Ruben, we are separated, so let me be."

Ruben did not want her to get off the phone and suggested that they go and see a movie. Sara respectfully declined the offer.

"I have some decisions to make about this marriage, and I have not made them. Please be respectful and allow me this time to be by myself."

"Fine, Sara! If that is what you want to do. Don't call me if you need anything."

"I won't!"

Sara hung up the phone and got upset about allowing Ruben to get her focus off. "He is not going to change," she said to herself. "Why did I set myself up for this? I should not have taken the call and let him get to me. Next time, I should not pick up the phone but rather let it go to voicemail or let him leave me a text if it is important."

She wanted this time away to reflect and think about her marriage and Ruben. She would hope that he took time to reflect on himself and his behavior, but she doubted that he would. He always wanted to pretend in front of his family, but when he was with her, he didn't treat her right.

Although Sara didn't have the best example of what a marriage is supposed be, she knew how she wanted to be treated and what she was willing and not willing to put up with. She stopped for a moment and took a deep breath, and asked God to give her strength. She turned up her Gospel music and continued to decorate. There was a knock at the door. Sara wondered who this could be. She wasn't expecting any company except Eduardo and Gustavo, who were out running errands, but she gave them the keys to get into her house. She went to the door and looked through the peephole; low and behold, it was Mel! She opened the door and gave Mel the biggest hug.

"What are you doing here, girl? I wasn't expecting you until the day of thanksgiving."

Sara's voice would always get high-pitched when she was excited, like her mom Sybil's. Mel informed Sara that she wanted to surprise her and how she missed her and the girls. She was so happy to see the woman who was and is a mom to her.

"I see you're decorating, Sara. Let me put my bags down and get out of these shoes and come help you."

Sara's friends were not the type of friends who just sat back and watched. They would ask what can they do? Need any help? If Sara said "No, I got it," they would help her anyway because they knew Sara needed help but knew she didn't like to ask. She asked

Sara where she wanted certain decorations to go and even gave her suggestions.

"I see your suitcase, but what are in the other bags asked Sara."

"You know I always have a gift for you and the girls. I knew Edwardo and Gustavo would be here and your parents, so I wanted to get everyone a gift. You know I am not like your in-laws and leave out people."

They both laughed.

"You know I always must hook my girls Autumn and Joy up." They are like granddaughters to me. Mel thought about it and then said, well, they are my granddaughters. Your parents and I adore Autumn and Joy very much. I know you do. They love you, Mel, and think of you as their grandma too. They will be ecstatic to see you. I hear you jamming out to I Got the Victory! Yes, girl. Sara began to tell Mel about the phone call she received from Ruben. She gave Sara some motherly advice about the situation, and anytime Mel talked, she knew that wisdom was speaking, so she soaked it in. The ladies continued to put the final touches on their decorations. They were just waiting for Gustavo and Eduardo to return from errands. They sat on the couch and watched some tv. They were talking about the show and in walks the brothers! They saw Mel and gave her a hug. Everyone was having a good time.

"When is Allison getting here?"

Eduardo asked.

"You know, I have not heard from her. I am going to have to call her and see. Knowing her, she will probably come the day of thanksgiving."

"Yea, she is always traveling. Must be nice."
Gustavo said jokingly.

"I would love to be able to travel like that one day. If I woke up and decided to go to Paris one day, I want to be able to hop up and go."

"That would be great! You will be able to do that sooner than you think they all said in harmony. Let's discuss the menu for thanksgiving."

"First, what are we going to eat for dinner tonight?"

Gustavo said.

"Do you all feel like dining in? or eating in? We can always have food delivered."

"Let's do that they said. I know you all have traveled to come and be with me, and I do appreciate it."

They began to look online to see what they wanted to eat. They were always eating, it seemed. Mel said, "We are a bunch of foodies."

They all laughed.

"I like trying new places to eat. There are so many different things."

They were telling each other what they wanted to eat, and Sara heard the doorbell ring. "Was that the doorbell?"

"I am not sure."

They all got quiet, and indeed it was the doorbell. Who could this be? I know my parents and the girls will be in tomorrow, and we have not heard from Allison. Sara went to look out the peephole, and guess who it was?

She yelled, "ALLISON! Oh my goodness, HI, beautiful. That is so crazy we were just talking about you."

"What? You all know I was going to sneak in."

"I was going to call you."

"Yeah, I wanted to surprise you all."

"Ha! What an awesome surprise. We thought you were traveling."

"I just got back from Ireland."

"What? How was that?"

"It was amazingly beautiful."

Allison said.

"It is a place that we all must go and visit. It was peaceful, and I didn't want to leave."

"Yes, let's go do that one day."

"Let's all go. We are trying to decide what we want to eat. Look at y'all always eating," Allison said and then began to burst into laughter.

"We are hungry."

As they were ordering their food, they began to reminisce on the good times; Sara would often daydreamed of a fairy tale wedding. She had what she thought was the wedding of her dreams, but the marriage not so much. She reflected on how she had always dreamed about her wedding and marriage as a little girl. She often thought that her spouse would treat her like a Queen. She never had to want for anything. She dreamed of her husband being a man chasing after God's heart, phenomenal provider, defender, and protector. However, she received the opposite. Although, she knows that there is no fairy tale marriage or perfect man, she had to learn to accept the things that she could not change.

It does not mean she has to stay in an unhappy and unhealthy marriage with her spouse. But she can talk to him and let him know what she needs from him. Boundaries are not to be mean, but they are to be healthy and respectful. You must take into account each other's feelings, and if you do not care how your spouse feels, then I am not sure how or why you are even married or in the relationship, to begin with. Spouses need to back each other up. You must be a team. If you are not a team, then you will always be at war with each other and with your extended family or others.

Sara did what she could to try and get her in-laws to see that she was not the person that Ruben told them about. Everyone that knew Sara knew was kind, sweet, thoughtful, beautiful, loving, and nurturing. However, her extended family did not believe that she was this type of person. They think Sara is mean, lazy, useless, uneducated, a street walker of the night, and a gold digger.

Every time she is around Ruben's family, they do not disappoint with their words and looks. The picture that was painted to them by Ruben is what they wanted to hold on to about her. They'd always try to act as if they loved her and were always happy to see her, but Sara knew the truth. Her mother n law had no shame in her game when she called Sara stupid. She doesn't hide how she really feels about her. She could not focus on that. She had to focus on Autumn, Joy, and finishing her education. She would go back and forth, reflecting on what they have said and done. Although she said she forgave them she was still in pain from the hurt they caused she and her daughter.

She thanked God that she had parents and friends pushing her to become all they knew she could be. She had a lot of late nights, coffee, tea, and she studied and worked hard because she knew if she was going to graduate in December, then she had to do what needed to be done. She had to make sacrifices.

Chapter 15

It was the morning of thanksgiving, and Sara's friends allowed her to sleep in. She woke up to good-smelling food in the kitchen. She loved her friends because they knew her so well and always cared for her and each other. She knew that Allison oversaw the vegetables because that is mainly what she ate. No, she wasn't Vegan; she rarely ate meat. Mel is making the dressing and mostly all the sides; Eduardo and Gustavo will be frying a turkey and roasting a turkey, she thought to herself. Before she headed downstairs, she said her prayers, took a shower, brushed her teeth, and put on her clothes. She was anxiously waiting for her parents and the girls to get home. She walked downstairs and said,

"Just as I suspected. I knew what each of you would be cooking."

She saw a breakfast spread that was well put together by Allison. It was very beautiful. "This looks so amazing, you guys! I truly appreciate each last one of you. You are dear to my heart," she told them.

They told her that she was loved. Just as she was going to go and fix her a plate with all the delicious breakfast food, the doorbell rang. Now, I know that's not my parents and the girls ringing my door when they have the key, she said. Sure, enough, it was! Autumn and Joy hugged their mother so tight and told her how much they missed her and were glad to see her. Mel and my parents were already talking and showing each other what they had gotten for my daughters to make sure they didn't get the same thing. They often kept in contact with each other because Autumn and Joy were their grandchildren. Mel began to shout, "May I have your attention, please?"

Everyone stopped what they were doing and looked at Mel. What announcement could she be making? She handed everyone a beautiful, wrapped card. Please open your cards everyone. We opened our cards, and it was an all-expense paid trip to PARIS! Sara could not believe her eyes. This was crazy! She just shared how she wished she could go to Paris someday, and now she doesn't have to worry about a thing. Tears began to fill her eyes, and Mel came over and hugged her tight and whispered,

"See, God answers prayer, he may not come when you want him, but our God is an on-time God. Happy graduation!"

Sara began to cry hysterically. She told Mel,

"I have not even graduated yet."

She said,

"I know, and I know you will walk across that stage come December."

Mel kissed her on the cheek and told her she had to get back into the kitchen to finish making all the sides. Everyone was too excited! There were screams, shouting, and dancing going on in Sara's house, and she loved every minute of it. Allison took out her phone and began to record everyone! Sara was so overjoyed because she wondered what she did to deserve such a good family and friends. With everyone so excited, Sara received a missed call from Ruben. This time she knew better than to answer the call. She kept the phone silent and continued the celebration with the others.

"Why is he calling me?" she thought to herself. "It is just like him to sense we are having a good time to try and break the fun. He should be with his family having fun, instead of calling me."

He then kept sending her text messages and wanted to see if Autumn and Joy could come and say hi to his family. She looked at her phone and knew very well, this was just one of his tactics for me to get to talk to him. He would use any and everything he could just so that I could respond, so he could then talk about other stuff. However, Sara was not falling for the tricks. She took this time to separate from him and his family, and that is exactly what she is going to do. She ignored the texts.

Thanksgiving had come and gone, and Sara was finally earning her bachelor's degree. By this time, she had one class to complete, and once that was done, she would officially have her degree. She could not be prouder of herself. Mel got the tickets for them to spend Christmas in Paris and let someone else do all the work so they could all relax, shop, eat, and have fun. When you are doing great things, here comes the enemy throwing any and everything your way to get you off track. Out of nowhere, one of Sara's friends came out of a bag on her. She wondered what in the world did she do to her? She was just minding her business and making moves for a better life for she and the girls. Sara felt she was being attacked not only from Ruben's family but her very own.

"What is happening?" She asked herself.

The family that she grew up in was supposed to support each other and be there for each other. However, her friend from high school, Jasmine told Sara that she was still in her 30's trying to get a college degree and how if she were to get remarried then she would have kids from different father's. What in the world was she talking about? Now, she had seen her a few months and they were talking about stories past and present. Why was Jasmine acting this way toward her?

In their discussion, Sara mentioned how Jasmine talked as if she was jealous of the help Sara had. Sara had help from her family, Ruben's family, and her friends. In that conversation, Jasmine asked Sara what does she have to be jealous of? Sara made it very clear that she didn't tell her she was jealous, but rather that's how she was acting, what a person fails to realize at times that your words hurt and can have a significant impact on a person, whether good or bad.

Sara was in disbelief that someone once so close to her could let those words be uttered out of their mouth. She assumed they were to lift each other and have each other's back. Let each other know how we felt and agree to disagree. Instead, this person decided to tear Sara down like Ruben's family would do. It was two days before Sara would walk across the stage to receive her degree. Why did this have to happen right before she was going to walk across the stage? I don't understand Sara said. Just when things are going well, then it's like you get knocked back down. Sara fired back at Jasmine and brought up things she had done. Jasmine didn't like that too well. One thing about Sara, people are starting to find out that she is not a pushover. Many people knew Sara to be a sweet and kind person. It's always easy to talk about what someone else has done or is doing, but when they fire back at you, people tend to get upset, and now you have become the wrong person.

They think they can bad mouth you because they think they have arrived. When they are going through, you are there for them, lifting them in prayer and encouraging them. As soon as they think they have arrived or are on top, they get around others and talk about the very one they are supposed to support. Your own family will put you down and talk mess behind your back. They can be very manipulative and have you thinking that you are the problem.

People in general will say one thing, and then when you confront them, they will turn around and say something totally different. They will play the blame game and never really take responsibility for their actions. These types of people you must be aware of and tread lightly. Sara didn't feel good for going off on Jasmine and apologized for how she hurt her feelings.

Jasmine never told her why she said such things, to begin with. The day Sara was to meet Ruben for lunch, she received a phone call from Jasmine.

"This is weird," she thought, "Why would she be calling me after saying such dreadful things about me?"

Nevertheless, she answered the phone. Jasmine apologized for saying those mean things to her and told her that she has not been herself lately. What she was about to tell her would furthermore damage their relationship. She began talking to Sara, about things that were happening in her life and her baby boy. Just before they were getting ready to hang up the phone, Jasmine told her that she slept with Bernard which is the guy Sara was dating back in college.

"You have got to be joking, right?"

She thought it was a dream. Surely this cannot be true. She wanted to scream, but instead, she asked Jasmine if she was 100 percent sure and when did this happen?

"How could you have had a relationship with the man that I was dating?

"The day I saw you at your aunts house , you and Bernard were talking then?"

This explains his behavior, and it explains your behavior.

"You and I were friends for a long time, and for you to do this to me is very wrong."

"What did I ever do to you? Was this your plan all along as to why you wanted to link up all all those years ago?"

Jasmine began crying, hoping Sara would have some sympathy for her, but it didn't work. She wanted Sara to know that she wanted them to be close like they used to be. Instead, Sara told her,

"You and I will never be close again, and she hung up the phone!"

It would soon be time to deal with Ruben about his late nights, controlling spirit, and his family. She needed to sit down and talk with him because she was unsure if she wanted to get a divorce or work through their problems. With the chaos from Ruben, Jasmine, and school, she knew she could easily just file for divorce from Ruben but at the same time she wanted to make sure she exhausted all her options before filing paperwork. Sara endured so much mental and verbal abuse from them. She started to think it was okay, and that's how they were, and she started to begin to accept it. She was in a dark and lonely place. Sometimes in the midnight hours, she would go pray and cry because of the hurt and pain in her heart. Sara was not only being hit by his family but her very own that she considered family. It was something that has not gone away easily from Sara's remembrance. Sometimes words that were spoken by the person who was close to her, tend to run through her mind every now and then. Sara often thought,

"Maybe she was too old to try and complete her college education, or maybe she wasn't college material."

Chapter 16

It came and went the words and memory of what happened, and she had to get right back up and go for what she set out to do. When you are abused, it can take a toll on your health. Here Sara was 35 and yet she found herself still struggling with what was said to her. It can be very difficult at times to remain focused because the negative words. No one knew the nights she cried or how she didn't sleep because of fear, worry, and pacing the floor all night long. She was dealing with a narcissistic husband, and so-called family was coming up against her. They didn't know the struggle except for Allison.

Allison always encouraged Sara and prayed for her and with her. She always pushed her and told her to keep going and fight for what she wanted. She was Sara's cheerleader. She was the only one who truly knew the extinct of what Sara was going through. The ladies were encouraging to each other because that was her best friend. They had each other and that is what they needed. They told each other their darkest secrets and they loved each other. The bond they have cannot be shaken. Many people have tried to come and destroy the friendship with gossip and lies. They tried to destroy it by causing division and getting the ladies to turn on each other. Sara and Allison knew when the enemy was at work. Yes, they have had disagreements and sometimes have gotten into screaming matches. However, when things were calm and they took a moment to themselves to reflect how awful they both behaved they always talked about where they went wrong and forgave each other.

Sara was getting discouraged and didn't feel like she could continue to press forward in achieving her goal to graduate. There was so much opposition that she was faced with and the sounds of negative words and people still ringing in her ear.   One day she was speaking with someone and they asked her how school was going. She didn't give them much information but the lady told her that if she kept going, she will finish. The piece of advice that was given to her may not seem like it is anything but to Sara, it was a light. The person told her even if you take one class at a time, keep going.

"If you don't stop, you will finish. If this reminds you of yourself, then DON'T STOP! KEEP GOING! Will it be tough at times?"

"Yes, prayer and perseverance will be needed for the journey. You will have to fight through all the negativity but whatever you do, Don't Quit! A support team will need to be in place. Someone you can talk to, and that will lift you up and not tear you down. To all of those that are in school getting their education or starting your business or whatever it is for you, I commend you! Keep going. For all of those who stopped, because life took some wild turns, I encourage you to get back up, dry your face off and finish. In the end, it doesn't matter who said what about you, or who wasn't there for you. No, it doesn't feel good but, take what was said or done and let it make you stronger. Let it push you towards your purpose and destiny."

If Sara had allowed what was said or done to stop her, she would still be in a state of stagnation. Sara got knocked down, and she was tired of the way things were going in her life. She wanted change, which is why she enrolled back into college to begin with. It was not just family and friends coming against her, her professors came up against her too. They didn't think Sara was college material and wanted her to quit school and join the military because she wasn't fit to be in school. She wasn't the smartest and they didn't think she could complete the college course that she was taken. Instead, they told her to go to a Junior college if she didn't want to go to the military.

The professors and president and vice president of the university didn't want her there. She didn't understand why they were coming up against her so hard. The university wanted to kick her out and not allow her to return. Sarah was distraught by this. She called her parents on the phone to let them know what the university president and their team were doing and saying. They didn't like the sound of this, so they made a trip and met with the president and spoke to them about their concerns.

The lady in the front office had the face of "go get them mom and dad." Before it was all over the results Sarah and her parents were looking for came to pass. Once she returned to school they did all they could to make sure that she was not going to graduate and that she would not return to the university. All of the things going on around her she still had to deal with the craziness of her husband. Ruben kept trying to give her a hard time. She knew sooner or later she and Ruben would need to sit down and talk about the state of their marriage.

He continued to call and text Sara all the time. One day, he texted her and she answered. He wanted to meet up with her for lunch. She agreed this time. She didn't know what Ruben wanted to talk about, but she knew that she was going to talk to him about their marriage. He asked her if it was okay for him to pick her up and she told him yes, that will be fine.

The day Sara was to meet with Ruben for lunch she had an uneasy feeling. She knew that they needed to talk. Just as she was about to do her hair, her phone rang. This is weird she thought. Why would Jasmine be calling me? After saying all of those dreadful things about me, then she has the nerves to call. Nevertheless, she answered the phone.

Jasmine apologized for saying those mean things to her and told her that she has not been herself lately. She began talking to Sara about how she felt bad for the things that she said and did. before they ended the call she told Sara that she loved her. Jasmine was still trying to win Sara over and wanted that close knit friendship they had. However, Sara still denied her. She didn't understand how Jasmine betrayed her like this, and they were best friends at the time who always hung out and had sleepovers. How could she do this to me?

All the times she said she was busy or couldn't hang out, and girl I got your back were a lie. This explains why she talked bad about me to Bernard to make herself look good and innocent and make me look like the bad one. This is why she wanted to be so close to me because she was after Bernard. It wasn't because she really loved me or even that she had my back, she just wanted what I had at the time Sara thought to herself.

Someone who was family would become the very one that would stab me in the back. Sara assumed she told her because she couldn't live with the guilt of knowing what she did to her. Why do I even care at this point? I am no longer with him Sara thought. She was more hurt that it was her best friend that did this to her. Sure, it could have been anyone but for your best friend to betray you that was on a whole different level. Sara reached out to Ruben and began to tell him everything Jasmine did and said. He replied "she is not welcome here." However, she knew she still had to deal with Ruben about he and his family's behavior. She had all these thoughts in her head and worrying about how to end it with Ruben or if she should stick and stay.

Maybe I should take my own car and meet him at the restaurant she thought. Or he can come here? No, I don't want him at my house she said. She tried to shake the feeling she had but she couldn't. She began to doze off and fell asleep. While she lay sleeping she began to have a dream and it was regarding she and

Ruben. The dream begins: It was 12:30 pm and Ruben pulled up outside of her home. She told him to call or text when he arrived. He did as he was told, and Sara got into the car, and off to lunch, they went.

They arrived at the restaurant and ordered their food and then Ruben began to make small talk. She wanted to wait for the perfect opportunity to bring up to him about possibly filing for divorce. However, there was no perfect time.

All the late nights that you were out, and all the late-night projects was that a lie Sarah asked, Ruben said, No! I really was out all night at the office working on projects and trying to get myself ready to present to my company why they should choose me for President of the corporation. That still doesn't excuse the fact that you stayed out all night and then I wouldn't see you until the next day. Ruben informed her that he would hang out with some friends too. Sarah informed Ruben that she was thinking about filing for divorce because his behavior was getting out of hand and he was way too controlling a lot of the times. She didn't want to be in that kind of marriage.

Ruben began to plead and beg with her not to and wanted them to work it out.

"Now, you want to save your marriage. You didn't think about your marriage when you were out in the streets. For crying out loud Ruben you allow your family to disrespect me and Autumn. You talk about us when they talk about us. You do nothing to stop this behavior and your always justifying their wrong. Would you want some man to treat your daughter how you treat me? This has been going on for way too long. You expect me to welcome them with open arms and act like nothing ever happened or anything was said. I cannot tolerate being around your family. They are some of the most fakest people I have come across. They only care about image, and you seem to be heading in that direction too. You only want me to go to things with you, so that they will not question you about us or make it seem as if our family is well put together when in reality it is not.

"Stop being fake with things!" She shouted. "I can no longer deal with disrespect, lies, or your family. This is too much for me."

Sara got up from the table and began making her way outside because she was going to call a cab. Ruben followed her and told her he'd take her home but that he wouldn't stop fighting for his marriage.

"We do not have a marriage anymore, Ruben can't you see that? This is over!"

They got into the car and began driving. However, she noticed Ruben driving a bit fast.

"Why are you driving so fast?"

"I am not driving that fast he told her."

"Ruben, if you are upset, then perhaps you should pull over so that I can drive." Ruben tuned her out and his driving increased.

"Slow down she shouted! Ruben! You are going to fast please slow down!"

He went to fast and the car they were driving flipped over a bridge and down they went. The ambulances came and many cars were stopped on the highway. You could hear more sirens coming in from a distance. She could hear someone asking her if she was ok.

"Ma'am. Stay with me a deep voice said."

"You have been touched by an angel another lady said."

How did Sara survive this nightmare? How is she not dead? Sara jumped out from the car and began to run for her life. She never looked back to see if Ruben made it out alive. She ran until she ran upon a little store where a little child was sitting in the floor eating her pastry. She and the little girl locked eyes. She was in the middle of nowhere. Yet somehow, this store was just here.

She can remember what the girl had on a pink and white dress. Her skin looked like caramel. She was such a beautiful girl. This girl seemed to be 3 or 4 years old. Why does she look familiar Sara said to herself? She asked the little girl if she could go get help. Sara laid on the floor and closed her eyes. The ambulance came and she again heard the deep voice of a man. This is a miracle several of them shouted! This was nothing but God that you survived! How do you wreck like that and began to get up and take off running with no bruises, scratches or broken bones? This is a miracle! The guy came over and put her on the stretcher and told Sara,

"We need to take you to the hospital to be sure there is no internal bleeding."

"Where is Ruben? He is my husband, and we were supposed to be getting a divorce. Where is he?"

"Ma'am, he passed away instantly."

Sara let out a loud scream and began to weep. She almost hit the floor, but the doctor grabbed her before she went down and sat her on the stretcher. "I am very sorry about your loss, ma'am. Do you think he was trying to kill you on purpose?"

"Yes, if he wasn't trying to kill me, then he wanted to make sure that I was harmed. He figured if he couldn't have me, then no one would be able to have me. I see God had different plans. I am truly blessed to be alive."

She began to weep, just thinking about how she survived the crash and how Ruben tried to kill her. She thought about everything that she had to do and how she needed to tell his family. How was she functioning in her right mind? The people of the small town of Velvet, TX, wanted to know how she was even in her right mind. How did this young lady survive flipping over a bridge going at an excessive speed? They were baffled by what they were seeing. All Sara kept hearing was that an Angel of the Lord was with her.

"Did anyone get his phone or my belongings at the scene?"

Yes, an officer will give you everything that is in the car once we get you to the hospital and evaluated. Is there someone that you can call to come with you?"

"Yes, I can call my friends. I don't want to worry my parents."

She unlocked her phone and began to dial Mel's number. She knew she didn't want to mess with Allison because she was always traveling, and Gustavo and

Eduardo were busy right now running their two businesses. Mel would be the only one that would have some free time since she was able to close her shop at any time. She got a hold of Mel and told her what happened, and Mel began to scream and went into panic mode. She wanted to know where to come to see Sara. When Mel arrived, she let the nurse know that she was her mother. She hugged Sara and began to cry because she could have lost a daughter.

"Have you contacted your parents?"

"No. Would you contact them and let them know that I am okay? I don't want them to have to drive down this late or worry about me."

The doctor came in and informed Sara that after doing some testing, they found no internal bleeding, and it was a blessing and a miracle to be alive after a crash like that. This is something that we cannot explain, the doctor told her. This was all Jesus Mel shouted! He protected her from danger, seen and unseen! Hallelujah! One thing about Mel, she will not care where she is or what she is doing, she is going to give God praise!

The doctor said, "AMEN!" He informed Mel that he would like to keep Sara overnight just for observation. She has been through something traumatic, and I just want her to rest. "Doctor, I hope that I can get out of here because I have a graduation to get to."

"Yes, I hope to have you out by tomorrow. All that you have been through, and you still make it to graduation?"

"Yes, I cannot let this stop me," Sarah said.

"I worked so hard to get to this day. I am feeling fine. I am just a little shaken, and I am in shock. However, I cannot allow that to stop me. I have been waiting on this day. I worked so hard to get to the finish line with my education. Although, I am sad, hurt, upset, and mixed with so many other emotions, I cannot allow this to stop me. Especially if I am feeling alright."

"You are a very tough lady and a blessed one too."

He smiled at Sarah and told her to get some rest and that he would come to check on her in the morning. Once the doctor left, Sara began to cry again. She was very hurt that Ruben passed away but angry that he tried to take her life with him. It is crazy how a person can be one way in front of you and your family and then another way behind closed doors. She started to let guilt sit in because she couldn't help but think that if she hadn't told him about wanting a divorce, then maybe he wouldn't be dead right now. She had to process everything that happened that day. She cried more and more because she knew she could have lost her life that day, but God said "NO"! How was she going to get through this storm? This was something else that the family would like to hold over her head.

Although, she survived, she was in pain and had to go to a lot of therapy. She also had her prayer warriors praying for her and with her. They knew that she couldn't bear this alone. That's the kind of friends she admired. She wouldn't wish this on her worst enemy to go through this. Sara woke up in a sweat and panic. She knew that the signs of abuse were there but didn't know to what extent. She knew that she should have gotten out when she could, but she disobeyed, and she paid the price for it. Mel, hugged Sara and held on to her tightly, because she heard her crying and began to pray for her. I don't want you to think any of this is your fault, because it is not. I want you to get some rest, and I will be right here when you wake up, Lord's willing. Rest Sara, you are going to get through this, she said. After a few weeks had passed by Sara began to prepare for her graduation.

Sara graduated on December 19th despite all that she went through. She had her family and friends there to cheer for her, and the whole gang celebrated her achievement. She wanted to break generational curses that held a lot of family back and begin to leave legacy for the generations to come. The most important thing she could do for her generation was to break the cycles and give them Jesus! That is one of the most precious gifts you can give.

Although, she didn't have much growing up, she had Jesus, and that was more than enough. She was glad her parents gave her that strong foundation, and that is what she gave Autumn and Joy and will give to anyone or other children she may have in the future, whether that is biological or non-biological. Sara began to change her way of thinking and doing things. She had to see herself better, stronger, healthier, and happier, and she began to look up resources and information to get her to where she needed to be. She took everything to God in prayer.

She told the Lord that she would do his will for her life instead of trying to do it her way. She told God, there is something that you want me to do as to why you allowed me to go through all that I went through. Even though some days were harder than others, she got back up in the fight and pushed herself. She keeps telling herself,

"Keep going, and don't stop until you have completed all your goals that you set out for yourself. People are going to talk and put you down and say all kinds of things. Let them talk! Keep going, keep pushing, and keep striving. This is your time!"

Sara went through a lot of hurt, pain, and betrayal. However, she didn't let those things stop her from what she wanted to do and where she wanted to be. It took her many years to heal, but she healed. She stayed separated from her husband for a few years. She knew she didn't want to get involved with someone right now because she was still married to Ruben and this would be wrong to do. She didn't want to divorce Ruben and then end up with someone who was like him or worse, and she didn't want to have to deal with in- laws that she had. Mrs. Mulberry would always say,

"Sara frustrated him and made him mad to the point he was tired."

This was all a falsehood. Even with she and Ruben not living together   she   still   believes what Ruben told her about Sara. With all that had been going on and taking time and years to heal, she finally healed and got over the pain, heartache, and loss. In the end, Sara made a decision to divorce Ruben. She didn't wan to show her daughters that this was acceptable behavior or that you had to put up with it just because other people think you do. You don't have to stay just because other people get into your head and make you think it is alright because you are not being physically abused. No! Sara did not want this for her girls.

She got remarried and allowed God to handpick the man for her this time. She has two beautiful girls and one handsome son. She is a firm believer the more negative (death) words you speak it will begin to manifest in your life. Your words can make or break you. You will have test and trials along the way, because these things must come. The Bible says in Ecclesiastes 1:1 *"to everything there is a season, and a time to purpose under heaven."*

When you hear negative words that have been spoken over you or someone you love, then you must cast those down and reverse it. If they   say, you are not beautiful, you say,

"I am fearfully and wonderfully made."

You must learn to take the negatives and turn them into positives. Sara was made fun of for being in her thirties and still no college degree. She had to turn it around and make a positive out of it. How many of you know that God's timing is not your timing? We cannot go by what man says ever! Always go by what God says, and you are who God says you are. Man is always going to have an opinion and say all kinds of things to you. Stand on what the word of God says about you! She started journaling more when she got re-married to talk about her life now and all that God has blessed her with. She began to write her visions down.

In Habakkuk 2:2-3 (KJV) says *write the vision, and make it plain upon the tables, that he may run that read it. For the vision is yet for an appointed time, but at the end it shall speak, and not lie; though it tarry, wait for it; because it will surely come, it will not tarry.*

Sara began to write visions, and even looking back over the years, she found some old journals and looked through them and realized how some of the visions she wrote began to manifest. You must have the faith to believe. For the Bible says in James 2:20 (KJV)

For the body without the spirit is dead, so faith without works is dead.

You must have faith! If it wasn't for those who made fun of Sara and put her down and talked about her it would not have made her stronger. Sara Bounced Back! She bounced back from all the negative words and bounced back from all the chaos and the devastation and the mistreatment of others. Why? Simple, because she did not give up! All the time that she wanted to give up on life and give up on God she never did. She had a strong foundation in Christ that her parents gave her. They gave her one of the greatest gifts which is Jesus! If it had not been for her foundation and her faith, then who knows what and where she would be today.

Chapter 17

Although you have been waiting and you want change now you can feel it all through your bones and often see yourself in a different light and not how others see you. Keep holding on and don't let go, do not let others persuade you or tell you that you cannot do it or that it will never happen. Sara had to do her part and heal and study and go through her trials and tribulations because in the end, the reward will be great! God says wait because it will surely come to past. Despite the haters and every tongue that rises against you, cast it down and reverse every negative word and keep it moving.

Matthew 6-15 (NKJV) lets us know that if we do not forgive a person of their trespasses neither will your Father forgive you. I am sure we have all had some things we had to go back and ask for forgiveness from the person/persons you did wrong. When people do something to us, we want to hold on to what they did or clap back at them waiting to get ready to throw hands. How dare they mistreat us? See we forget how we have mistreated people. I don't know about you, but I don't want to hold on to grudges or un-forgiveness and have my Heavenly Father not forgive me.

Can you imagine Jesus not forgiving you? I just do not want to imagine that at all. Yes, it is hard to forgive sometimes but you must do this! Your destiny depends on it. Even if the other person never tells you they are sorry, forgive them anyway, Sara had a hard time dealing with forgiveness with her husband and his family, she had to let go of hurt from a relationship she was in and her best friend at the time had sexual interactions with her ex-boyfriend.

She felt so betrayed, and this was a knife in her heart, and she never experienced this kind of heart until that very moment. Yes, it was very hard to forgive them, but she knew she had to do this. Make no mistake it was hard because she would get in her feelings at times and say, remember what they did or said? Or if they did something or said something it would bring up memories. You should not allow a person to continue to mistreat you. Learn when to walk away from someone that is mishandling you.

If you must separate yourself for a while, then do that. If you choose to work things out between you and your spouse and decide to stay together, then that is your business. Sometimes you have to walk away for a moment and then come back together. Make sure you come back stronger, healthier, happier, and in agreement with each other. Make sure you do the work you need to do to fix the relationship and make the necessary changes should you decide to work it out.

Stick up for yourself and do it in a way that it is not violent or hurtful to you or the other party. Often times, we say things that we can't take back and hit them where it hurts. Words do hurt! Sometimes, it may be best to just stay silent, because that speaks volumes. Dust yourself off and keep it moving. You do not have time to worry about what they are doing or saying because you can Bounce Back from the situation you are in. Let's forgive one another and heal so we can begin to move on with our lives, so that we can get all of what God has for us. Moving on with your life doesn't require you to go back to the very thing or the very one that hurt you. If they choose not to forgive you, then move on anyway and let the healing begin so that you can head towards your future and destiny.

It wasn't easy for Sara, but she had to mature and grow in her faith and in her life in general to be able to see things differently. Her reaction to things that have been said about her or done to her is much different than what it used to be. She prayed, and she did the work, Thank you, Jesus!

You must remain focused because you are bouncing back from all the hurt, from all the distractions, pain, and setbacks. Bounce back because you can make it! You are not in this alone, you have a friend in Jesus (John 15:15.) If Sara can bounce back anyone can bounce back! There are many of you, who will go back and finish school, work on your business plan, or work on projects you laid to the side, what you started, finish regardless of what others have said or may say, finish regardless of the fiery test and trials you may face, It does not matter what it looks like to others as long as you finish.

I pray that God puts a finisher's anointing on your life, to finish what you have started, it is not too late. God can redeem the time that was lost, Sara used to think that she was too old, and that it was too late for her. The devil is a liar! With what once took you years to do, will now take you weeks or months. Drown the outside noise and voices (negative words.)

Focus on the task that you want to complete and give God all the glory! This did not come easy for Sara. However, she can identify the enemy and tackle him head on and shut his mouth. For the Bible says in II Corinthians 2:11 for we are not ignorant of Satan's devices. Let me encourage you and tell you that It Is Not Too Late! I understand that you may not know how this will happen or when this will happen and may not even be sure how to get your resources, but all things work together for good to them that love God, to them who are called according to his purpose (Romans 8:28 KJV).

I understand it gets frustrating, and you want to quit. I understand that what you're going through does not add up to the promises that God has spoken over your life, the devil wants you to think that your life is over and that it will never happen. The enemy wants you to believe that the promises of God are null and void, you serve a miraculous God, a miracle working God, a promise keeping God and he can do anything and he can change anybody and any situation around; He can take your circumstances from jacked up to putting you in places you never thought you'd be in and being all that he has called you to be in a split second! All it takes is one word.

All it takes is one touch from God to make a change in your life. That is just how our Jesus rolls! There was days Sara couldn't see how the promises of God were going to work out in her life. He had shown her some great things and has told her some great things. However, she was once like you. How in the world is this going to work out? You see, it is not our job to figure out how, when, or where. Jesus has already figured that out for you. If you just begin doing what he has told you do, he will begin to open the doors and put you before great men or women and will direct your path and put you together with your destiny links. Those Godly links are people that have been called "specifically to you." Those are your friends, that are not jealous of you and can pray for you and with you, your I got your back when your around and when you're not around type of friends/destiny links.

For we know that God is the ultimate true friend. He will send you those who are real and not fake, those that will already be on it without you having to tell them to do this or that or I need this. There is nothing impossible for him to do in your life. We may think it is impossible because of what we see and what we are going through. The God that delivered the Israelites out of Pharaoh's hand (Exodus 5:1-23 KJV) and the God that delivered Shad Rack, Meshach, and a Abednego (Daniel 3:16 KJV) is the same God who can and will deliver you out of your situation. This is the time you Bounce Back! Don't you dare sit where you are and let the devil tell you that it's not worth it or that you might as well give up, or it's just a dream?

The devil is the father of lies! I am here to tell you that you will Bounce Back. Bounce Back from the hurt, lies, abuse, depression, or whatever it may be. You will overcome this. You must keep fighting, pushing, and believing God. If Sara had not bounced back from all that she went through, she would still be where she was, which is stuck, depressed, lonely, and wanting to give up on life. Do not be that person. In the book of Psalm verse 30:5 KJV it says,

Weeping may endure for a night, but joy cometh in the morning.

Hold on, brothers and sisters, because joy is coming! It won't be long now. Don't give up, don't give in, don't bow down to the enemy. Keep going. If you keep going, you will finish, and you can accomplish all that you set out to do. Yes, there will be tough times, trying times, hard times, and at times you will want to give up. DON'T. You are not what your naysayers say. You are who God says you are, If God has spoken it, then that settles it, God's word will not return void (Isaiah 55:11)

Everything that Sara wanted and more she received. She wanted a loving husband and in- laws, and she was beginning to see things come to pass that she had written down in her journal. She is still the best of friends with Allison, Mel, Eduardo, and Gustavo. The friends stay in contact with each other and often travel together. They still host dinners or lunches. Sara and her new husband Ryan welcomed their newborn baby boy and her friends welcomed their nephew and had the biggest baby shower for Sara and her husband. She still could not believe the joy and happiness that she found. She thought maybe this was a dream, but it was reality and she got more than what she prayed for. She often looks back where she came from and all that she had to endure to get to the place she is now.

How can someone have all the evidence in front of them and still not believe it? Although saddened about her ex-in-laws and how they would never see her or get to know her for who she is, she was glad that she and her husband have a healthy marriage and she is happier than she has ever been before. How can someone have all the evidence in front of them and still not believe it?

Never did she or the family tell Sara sorry or how they were devastated by how their son treated her and the lies they believed. No, they just liked to keep everything swept under the rug. They thought they could continue to belittle Sara and talk trash about her, and she would keep ignoring it and go around them and hangout out, knowing fully well they do not like her and Autumn. He tried to kill Sara in her dream, yet somehow the mother would accuse her of being the one to blame because she believed Sarah made him do it.

For everything wrong that happened, Sara was to blame. She was to blame for things not going well. In her mind, she believes she woguld frustrate him so terribly; that's why he would do or say what he said. Other times Sara would hear them talking about her or having phone conversations about her, and the whole time Mrs. Mulberry would put her down. One day Ms. Mulberry accidentally dialed Sara's number, not knowing that Sara picked up the phone and heard everything she said.

She was talking to Mr. Mulberry about her, and he kept telling Karen to let it go, but she refused and kept on talking.

Finally, Mr. Mulberry says, "Karen, your phone, your phone is on!"

Sara told her that she could hear everything she said, and she told Sara, "Good!"

Not once did Mr. or Mrs. Mulberry apologize to her for all the damage that was done or the things that were said. They knew, or I should say Ms. Mulberry tried to smooth it over with gifts, food, and money. They knew they had done wrong but did not want to admit they were wrong because Ms. Mulberry always has to think that she is right and she knows everything. It is her way or the highway. It goes to show you that some people never change. She bid them farewell.

At this point, Sara did not care because she had her own car she continued working on herself and working on some projects that she had put to the side. She didn't want anything to do with Ruben's family, or Ruben for that matter. She wanted to maintain her peace.

In the divorce hearing, Ruben tried to make Sara look bad and explained to the judge how she didn't with this or that and that she would just spend his money. He tried to make it as if she was lazy and a horrible mother.

Ruben was always good with playing the victim and hero. He always played the hero when his family was around and made Sara out to be the negative and bad one. However, the court saw things differently and awarded Sara with everything that Ruben had except the clothes on his back and his house. His mother was so angry.

Sara remembers when Mrs. Mulberry told her that she would not bankrupt her son. Now, Sara didn't have to bankrupt him and was being very generous but her lawyer stepped in and told her, No, we are going to get what you deserve and then some. Allison was there to support Sara every step of the way.

One thing about Allison she didn't take any mess and especially when it came to her family. Sara told Mrs. Mulberry her that she'd pray for her. She never considered Sara's feelings or even wanted to sit down and have a talk with her. Sara told Mrs. Mulberry You, not one time told me that your sorry, but you think that I owe you an apology. I really hope you can move forward and get the hate out of your heart.

Sara walked off along with Allison, and she went to the car and begin to cry her eyes out. Although all that happened with Ruben and the dream she had was a constant reminder of what could have happened to Sara she knew she had to do what was best for her and the girls. The enemy wanted to take the both of you out, but God had a different plan for your life and allowed you both to live. Now, you must tell the world your testimony Sara.

Yes, I hate this happened to you, but it was for a purpose. She gave Sara a hug, and they drove home. They tried to fight her every step of the way but each time God came through for her. Of course they were mad! However, Sara did not really care about that.

One thing she wasn't going to do with them is argue and fight. Those days were over for her. She no longer cared what they thought about her or how badly they talked to her. She didn't care if they tried to speak ill will of her or speak death words over her life. None of the things they tried to do worked. You see, she was blessed beyond measure.

They couldn't stop the plan and call of God on her life. They tried, but it failed at every turn. Their plans to ruin her life did not work out how they thought it should. They thought if they could ruin her life how they thought she ruined Ruben's then that would make them feel better. What would that get them? That still wouldn't make the plan of God for her life go away.

Often people think they have to get you before you get them, or if I make your life miserable and do what you did to me, then it will make you feel better. However, it will not. You will still feel miserable. We have to learn to let things and people go that are not good for us.

You see, Sara did not want to let go and wanted to hold her marriage together as long as she could. Although this was a dream that felt like reality, she knew that this is what could happen to her if she wasn't obedient and moved when God said to move.

Sometimes, God has to allow things to get uncomfortable and shake some things up to get you to move or he will move them for you. When you're in the storm or situation it doesn't feel good. How many of you know that storm is to make us strong and that these trials and tribulations must come and push us toward or destiny. If you have been in Sara's shoes, then you know how it feels. When we are disobedient God cannot move how he wants to move. Sometimes, he allows you to sit in the mess for a little while to help you realize that what you wanted is not what you needed.

When she was ready to leave, she couldn't make any moves until God got ready to allow her to get out of the situation. Once she was able to separate herself, she had time to herself and to think about what she wanted to. You may need to get away from all the voices in your ear and be still and hear the voice of the Lord. Jesus will not fail you like man will. He won't confuse you like man will because he is not the author of confusion I Corinthians 14:33 KJV.

Now Sara goes around the world on speaking engagements encouraging and helping men and women. The life she prayed for is the life that is starting to manifest between her and Ryan. She is living with her husband, and they have a new baby boy. Zachariah comes from a good loving home. She never thought that she would find love again. She continued counseling even after the divorce because she wanted to continue to work on herself and not repeat the same cycles. Does she and Ryan have disagreements? Yes, they do, but they know how to talk through them without being mean and hateful toward each other.

Are the in-laws any better, you may ask. They are great! She wanted loving, caring, patient, praying in-laws and she got just that and more. Ruben's family is still holding Sara to what Ruben said about her. She doesn't care if they talk about her, but she will not tolerate blatant disrespect from them. She will only say hi to them if she sees them in passing. After all, they have nothing to talk to about. Every time they see Sara, they ask the same questions over and over again.

They are more careful to speak because they don't want to offend Sara. Layla has learned to call Autumn beautiful, too, and Mrs. Mulberry is the one that you still have to watch. She is still mean and hateful not only to Autumn but to Rachel's girls too. We continue to lift that woman up in prayer. All that Sara had to endure and go through, she thought this was God punishing her for her disobedience.

She went through so much hurt and pain, until she didn't think there was any hope for her. She thought to herself, how can one person go through so much and still come out in their right mind and still serve God? Like, she thought her life was over and that she'd be alone forever or that she'd be in the grave. She didn't realize what she knows now. She understood that all she went through was not just for her, but it was to help others that may be in her situation or going through it now, to help them and know that there is a way out.

She had to endure all this pain and hardship only to realize what she went through was the blessing in disguise. She wasn't looking for love in all the wrong places nor was she in and out of relationships anymore. She didn't want to keep jumping in and out of relationships after what she went through. She really wanted to give up on relationships at that point in her life because of what she had been through. Any issues she had with anyone, she learned to take it to God in prayer.

Sara loved that she and Ryan's family could take vacations together and eat together in peace, laughter, and joy. She also loved that both sides of the family got along with each other when they came to visit us. She and Ryan are now in the process of getting the home that Sara always wanted. She didn't get a say so when she and Ruben married because he already had the house. He didn't want her ideas or her style in his house. Ryan prayed for Sara and prayed for the children, and they prayed together as a family. She just couldn't believe that this is the life she was now living.

He was more involved with the children and attended all of their activities. She didn't feel as though she had to walk on eggshells around Ryan or that she couldn't be herself with him or her in laws. She enjoyed not having to fight her battles because Ryan always had her back and defended her. This was very different for her, and she had to learn to embrace the love that God had sent to her.

Shortly after she and Ryan married, he adopted Joy and Autumn. This was something that Autumn would have loved for Ruben to do, but she started to see his true colors and didn't want to be adopted by him. Sara was never going to force her daughter to be adopted by any man. Autumn was old enough to make that decision if she had wanted him to adopt her. She wanted this to be a choice that Autumn made. Sara continues to uplift others and write in her journal. She wants to be able to help other people that may be going through this situation now. Maybe your saying to yourself, there is no way out? How do I get out of here. I just want you to know that there is a way of escape. There is a way out.

In *Deuteronomy 31:6 (KJV) it says, Be strong and of a good courage, fear not, nor be afraid of them: for the Lord thy God, he it is that doth go with thee; he will not fail, nor forsake thee.*

You see, you may be going through right now but hold on. I know it doesn't feel good and that you may feel lonely at times. Trust me, God has got you. If he had Sarah and held her up and gave her everything new and double for her trouble, then surely he will do the same for you. You may feel alone, but you are not alone. Sara was in a time in her life that she felt at her lowest to the point she didn't even want to be here on earth anymore.

The devil wanted her mind to run her crazy, but she kept holding on to God's hand. There were times she wanted to let go of it, but she kept holding on. She knew, if she kept holding on to his hand, that God would surely pull her out of the mess she got herself into. You see, the signs and warnings were all around her to get out of a situation that God saw, but she didn't. He warned her through people and things, but she didn't listen.

Some of you may have ignored the signs too, and now you are going through a hard time. Do not give up on God because he is not giving up on you. It's not to say that you will go through the same thing that Sara went through because everyone has their path and journey that they must take to get to where God is trying to take them. This was Sara's journey she had to go on. Jesus graced her to get through the trials and tribulations that she endured so that she could come out on the other side better and stronger.

He gave her joy for her mourning. The Bible says in Psalms 30:5 (KJV) *that For his anger endure the but a moment; in His favor is life; weeping may endure for a night, but joy cometh in the morning.*

Yes, there will be weeping, but it will not last. As the song says by Timothy Wright, "Trouble don't last always." What you're going through will not last always. It is for a moment, but it will leave, and you will smile again, you will have joy again, and you will have peace! Sara thought what she went through was in vain. She didn't realize that she would be helping others who are going through similar situations. If you are going through this, I am here to tell you to hold on. Do not give up! You may have to scream or cry, and that is alright.

There were days and nights Sara had to do this very thing. She would sometimes go to her car and scream because of what she was dealing with. She told God how she couldn't take anymore. Her hair was falling out to where she began to go bald in some spots of her hair, her health was failing, she would go and hide in her closet a lot and cry.

She didn't want Autumn to see the tears fall from her face, nor did she want Ruben at the time to see them. She was good at masking all her emotions. If you were not close to her, then you really weren't able to pick up on certain things, like her close family and friends were able to. Allison could always tell when something was wrong with her.

Nevertheless, Sara still held on to her faith! She didn't let go and trust me, she could have, but she had seen God bring family members out of dark situations and friends out, so she knew he would do it for her. She saw her best friend Allison go through some stuff, but he always came through for her. She wouldn't know if she could afford food, let alone her light bill, but God came through for her right on time. Sara would say, "God, if you just get me out of this, then I will leave."

However, she stayed in a tough situation for seven years before she was able to break free. She was in a situation where she didn't have anyone to help her at the time, nor could she go and stay with anyone. It was like everyone she knew that she could get help from, were not able to help her. She sat there and suffered and relied on her faith in God to pull her out. When he did open that door, she took off.

She got her and Autumn, and Joy out of that toxic environment. No, it wasn't easy for her because she was uprooting not only herself but her children from the only place they ever knew. She managed to keep her babies in the same school, but it is tough to have to uproot your family. She had to make a decision.

Do I stay in this toxic environment and keep enduring abuse or do I get out and get my peace of mind? She chose peace over a toxic relationship and environment. One thing she didn't want to teach Autumn and Joy was to stay in abuse. She didn't want them growing up doing the same thing. She wanted to show them and even some family members what it looks like to leave a situation. She found a lot of the women stayed because of the children. Others stayed even though they were being abused verbally and physically. However, she began to see the pattern and knew that she couldn't stay.

She was so used to being abused that she thought that was love because that's all she knew her whole life. No matter how she tried to get men that were not abusive, they would always end up being abusive verbally. This is not the lifestyle she wanted.

Chapter 18

She made a choice to get out! If you are staying for the children, then you are staying for the wrong reason. I know that you may want to keep your family together. Is it worth you getting abused? Is it worth your health failing? Is it worth it mentally? Are you staying just for convenience, hoping that it will get better? These are all questions Sara had to ask herself. One thing about children they will adapt to wherever you take them. No, it may not be what you want or where you want to live, but you must decide. Nobody deserves to be abused. You do not have to stay in a situation that you don't want to be in. You can make it! It's one thing if you decide to work things out with your spouse, but that is between you and your spouse.

However, if you find that you are working on it and they still choose to treat you like garbage, then ask yourself, is it worth it? See, Sara went to counseling and jumped from counselor to counselor and found that they could not help her. It wasn't necessarily the counselor; it was who she was in counseling with. Her boyfriend (Ruben) at the time went, but it would go in one ear and out the other. He never did what the counselor told him to do. This went on for years, and finally, Sara had enough and told him that she wasn't going. It wasn't working. He wasn't ready to change, and she wasn't willing to wait on him. She wanted to get on with her life, and that is exactly what she did. I know it will not be easy, but your peace of mind is worth it. To be in a place of your own and not have to have fights or arguments or go hide and cry, it is worth it.

Do not stay in something when you know God is telling you to leave that situation. If God is telling you to leave and you know you should leave, then leave. He is not going to tell you to do something and then not see that you have everything you need. Sara didn't know how in the world she would make it by herself. Her income wasn't that much, and she didn't even know how she would get furniture. However, God made a way for her each time. Some of her family couldn't understand why she moved out or thought she may have made the wrong decision. Some didn't even believe that God told her to go and that it was okay for her to stay because he wasn't abusing her physically. Abuse of any kind is wrong!

She is writing and encouraging other people that may be in the situation to know that there is hope and that there is a way out. If she got out of a bad situation and God blessed her with more than what she asked for, then you can too. She knew that this was a blessing in disguise. She now knows that she had to go through all of this to get to the other side. To get to her peace and a place of forgiveness, to get to her happy place. The things that she has prayed for continue to be manifested even now.

Once she got out of that place and in a place of obedience, God continued to move in her life. Yes, she is still helping and encouraging others because of all of what she went through and to be able to come out on top is the blessing in disguise. She didn't think that all of what she went through would bring her to her destined place. She could not fathom it. She would receive prophecies over her life but didn't think they would actually come to fruition.

It wasn't until she started being obedient and being led of God and not her emotions that she began to see them manifest. I encourage you to keep on going no matter what it may look like or sound like, no matter who's talking about you or coming up against you. Sara didn't realize that with all she had been through that, she would find purpose in her pain.

If you keep going and continue to be obedient, to God, you, too, will begin to see the blessings of God in your life. She now has leaders that look out for her well being and that push her to do things that she was afraid to do because of fear and what other people may say. She wanted leaders that she could trust and that didn't preach what she told them across the pulpit. She got leaders that pray for her and with her, support her, and tell her when she is wrong with love and kindness. Sara continues to speak blessings over not only her but her children, husband, household, and her family.

Speak affirmations and blessings over your life. Write them on a sticky note and post them on your mirror or wherever you see fit. Say them every day!

1. You are more than a conquer.

2. God has a plan for my life.

3. I will be all that God has called me to be.

4. I will not lack because God provides for me

5. I am beautiful/handsome.

6. I am loved.

7. I am smart.

8. My household will thrive and never lack.

9. I am a money magnet.

10. I am a wealth carrier.

Speak it and believe it! No matter what you are going through or have been through, there is a blessing in disguise when life takes a turn for the worst.